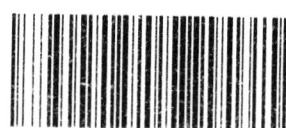

THE ALTAI

Also by Tony Frank

OUTAGE
THE LESSER OF EVILS

All Rights Reserved. Copyright © 2018 Tony Frank

No part of this book may be reproduced or transmitted in any form or by any means, graphic, electronic, or mechanical, including photocopying, recording, taping or by any information storage or retrieval system, without permission in writing from the author.

Printed in the United States of America

The Altai is a work of fiction. Any resemblance to actual events or persons, living or dead, is entirely coincidental.

Prologue

The World Has Lost a Magnificent Phallus.

Because the headline and its related article appeared in one of London's Arabic-language newspapers, it raised only a select few Anglo eyebrows. Two readers, one at MI5, Britain's domestic intelligence agency, the other at MI6, the foreign intelligence counterpart, caught it because it was their job to scour the contents of such publications every day. They were also required to cull and translate those articles considered to be of possible interest to the intelligence analysts. Though this particular piece did not fit in that category, it did elicit a few hearty chuckles. It was also noticed by seventy-two-year-old Jane Lambert as she brewed a kettle of tea in her house in Chiswick, on London's western fringe. She laughed out loud at the headline, noted that the author was a renowned female Kuwaiti dissident residing in London, and read the narrative.

"Oh, my," she murmured wistfully, "the old Emir's gone and died!"

As if on cue, the kettle whistled.

The folded newspaper was jammed under Jane's arm when she carried the tea tray to her living room. She set both down on a side table and ran a finger across the bindings of photo albums on a bookcase until she found the one she was looking for. She took it to her favorite chair next to the bay window overlooking the Thames. Wishing her husband were still alive so she could share this news with him, she poured herself a cup of tea and opened the album.

The first few pages contained photographs of the two of them together in 1968, shortly after they had first arrived in Kuwait as a couple. Posing in a stark desert landscape with a herd of camels in the background…his Land Rover in front of the Quonset hut that had served as the falcon hospital in those early days…the two of them sharing a laugh with friends from the Anglo-American Kuwait Oil Company, the revenues of which had already started to transform the country…the sun rising over the gulf to the east, setting over the sandy horizon to the west. In a way, the news of the day closed the circle on one of the most bizarre episodes of their twenty-four years together in Kuwait. She reflected on how uniquely positioned they had been to learn the details of what had happened. Now this, a final footnote.

Taking a sip of the tea, she reminisced about the most extraordinary series of events that had transpired in the autumn of her first year in her husband's homeland. It was inevitable that she would now replay everything over in her mind, as she had done so often, only today it would be with a heightened sense of closure.

She turned the pages of the album until she found the first photograph of the creature that had started it all. In monochromic majesty, regal of posture and imperious of gaze, the Altai.

Chapter One

The flutter was brief, yet fatal. A single flap of the wings, a futile lurch for freedom.

Far overhead, a falcon coasting on a morning thermal registered the movement, locked onto the source, swept its wings back and plunged.

The fettered pigeon was oblivious, preoccupied with the tether around its leg. In the sky above it, earth's fastest creature plummeted, now at close to two hundred miles per hour. Yet there were uncharacteristic shudders in its stoop, departures from the normal straight-line trajectory, adjustments that suggested to the keen eyes holding vigil that something was amiss.

Two blinks before impact, the invisible man twitched. He jerked the string up from his groin, across his chest and over his shoulder. The pigeon dug its claws in the desert sand, to no avail. Yanked by the string, it slithered unknowingly into the death zone. In an instant the falcon checked its arc and thrust out its own claws, these bigger, sharper and stronger, raking its hook-like rear talons into the pigeon's back. Blood spouted amidst a flurry of wings and feathers as the falcon clamped its beak around the pigeon's neck and cleanly severed its spine.

In the hunting blind, the man's patience was practiced, his timing exquisite, the latter a sign that at nineteen years of age, he was a natural. With a flick of his wrist he released the net and it sprang up and over both birds in a blur of motion perfectly choreographed to the falcon's strike. He swept aside the palm fronds concealing him and leapt out of his hole. He ran to the net, stoked by the thrill of success.

It was a remarkable specimen, a female, for no male could be this big. Its immature plumage—the brown wing and tail feathers were longer than a mature adult's—delighted him. It would be easier to tame, and he was not depriving the wild population of a breeder by trapping it.

"*Khosh farkh,*" he murmured. *Fine callow bird.*

As the falcon lashed out at the net, the man's eyes zoned in on the bird's dark brown iris, his gaze grounded in admiration and respect. Hunter, beholding hunter now prey. Again the falcon flailed. Agitated prey. He had to move fast to sedate it before it hurt itself. He reached into his pocket for a suture pack and tore it open. Grasping the falcon under one arm just tightly enough to immobilize it, he deftly passed the needle through the center of its lower eyelids. He pulled the free ends of the thread up to draw the eyelids shut and tied the ends over the falcon's head. Suddenly blinded, the falcon thrashed no more.

The man could scarcely believe his luck. This one was unlike any falcon he had ever seen. It was bigger, more imposing, surely more deserving than any other of the moniker, *Queen of the Skies.* And darker, too. Was this a *Sinjari?* It fitted the description, but they were so rare he had never seen one, so he couldn't be sure. Regardless, this bird was going to elevate him from obscurity to the ranks of the elite falconers. He would have to train it, of course, but that would only take two weeks, perfect timing for the start of the hunting season.

Riding a rush of adrenaline, he scrambled down an escarpment to the pickup truck parked in the gulley below. He grabbed his *subuq*, the leather tethers he would fasten around the falcon's ankles, and his *mangalah*, the camel hair-padded, fabric-covered cuff that would protect his hand and wrist from the falcon's sharp talons when he carried it. Essentials in hand, he scampered back up the ridge.

Now, with the falcon still, he noticed that two of its wing feathers were broken, likely the reason for the erratic corrections he had witnessed during its stoop. A minor blemish, surely a routine repair job for the English doctor. Best to get the hawk to her right away; the sooner it was restored to perfection, the sooner he could start training it. With the falcon on his arm and a spring in his step, he was walking on clouds as he made his way back to the pickup truck.

It was a fifteen-minute drive through the desert to Magwa, the shantytown he called home. He skirted around Ahmadi, the oil town with the prefab houses sporting gardens of trimmed grass lawns and eucalyptus trees, where British and American employees of the Kuwait Oil Company lived with their families. He circumvented the Bechtel-managed construction site of the North Ahmadi Tank Farm, where his father had found temporary employment as a night-shift security guard. It was sprouting massive steel tanks that would soon store crude oil piped through from gathering centers before being transferred to one of the local refineries, or to tankers at the shipping terminals. In recent times past, when he would return from the hunting blind empty-handed, the drive would be one of bitter reflection on the injustices of the world around him. He would dream of being an engineer and working in oil production, instead of being illiterate and unemployed. But today was not for the usual bile. He remembered his mantra: *I may be without much, but I am not without hope.* A glance at the creature on the passenger seat next to him brought a smile to his face. Today was for elation the like of which he had never known.

Mid-September meant it was still summer, a few weeks yet to go before October brought with it cold, dry, northwesterly winds from the middle of Asia, and before thundery fronts dropped the temperature and autumn rains spawned new leaves on the shrubs and salt bushes that now looked emaciated. Perennials dotted the arid landscape, their roots stretching farther into the earth to draw water from a greater depth than those of the annuals. The monotony of the undulating plain was broken by the occasional hill or shallow depression that, with the winter rains, would become a watering hole for the bedouin camel herds.

A few minutes past the tank farm, around a set of dunes sculpted northeastward by the prevailing winds, Magwa came into view. A slum dissected by one two-lane blacktop that ran north-south from Ahmadi to the airport, it consisted of hundreds of thatch-walled shacks with corrugated iron roofs. And dominating it from atop the rise on its northern edge, the large Quonset hut, the man's immediate destination. The sight of it brought a pang of trepidation, the familiar fear of rejection that beset him whenever he approached anything that smacked of officialdom or governmental authority. He lived not two minutes away, yet he had never been inside. Ever since the British had erected it, it had been primarily a maternity clinic, so a no-go zone for him in more ways than one. But with the recent completion of the oil company's new hospital down the road in Ahmadi, the hut had been transformed into the country's first falcon hospital. That had been, as everything that materialized quickly in the country, by decree of the Emir, himself an avid falconer, and the ultimate symbol of officialdom and authority.

He followed the dirt road into Magwa, pulled up at the shack he called home, and let out a short, distinctive tongue whistle, one he had learned from herding sheep. A boy came running out of the neighbor's shack.

"Hamza!" the man said, "Come see!" He noticed another movement in the shadows of the shack, the one he was hoping he would see, and his heart fluttered. Hissa, the boy's sister, was watching. He could only see her because she wanted him to. She drew forward so the sun lit her face. He could see her eyes, so he knew she saw his smile.

The boy ran to the Datsun, and the man picked the falcon up off the floorboard so to show it off.

"Aieeee!" the boy erupted. "It is unbelievable!" He looked at the man reproachfully. "Why didn't you take me with you?"

"It was too early. I left before sunrise. I think it is a *Sinjari!*"

"*Sinjari!*"

"But look, it has some broken feathers. I will take it to the hospital, to the English doctor; she can mend them."

"Take me with you!"

"No, you stay here. I will call you when I return."

He glanced again at the shack. Hissa was still there, and to his utter delight he saw that his smile was reciprocated, albeit furtively, but that was all right, for it was the only way it could happen, and only for the briefest of moments.

The Datsun kicked up a contrail of dust as it meandered around the shacks and cut a trail towards the Quonset hut. The man leaned on the horn to scare a donkey out of the way, before skidding to a stop at one end of the semicircular corrugated galvanized steel structure. He had deliberately not shown his father the falcon, for it was mid-morning, and the old man would be asleep. Besides, he wanted his wondrous raptor restored to perfection before showing it off to his father, from whom he had learned everything he knew about falconry.

The sign above the door read "FALCON HOSPITAL" in English and Arabic, but it only reinforced his angst by reminding him he was illiterate. He was relieved to see that the only other car there was that of the English doctor. The Morris Wolseley was distinctive because it was a right-hand-drive car in a left-hand-drive country, an oddity not lost on the locals. He had seen her driving it hither and to a few times. The novelty of a solo woman driver had initially created a buzz in Magwa, but it soon became known that she enjoyed a special status, an immunity of sorts, on two counts: First, she was the wife of Abdul-Razzaq Yassine, the doctor who worked for the oil company, noted for being the first Kuwaiti to get a medical degree from a British university. Second, upon meeting her at a function in honor of her husband and learning that she was a bird doctor by schooling, the Emir himself had decided to establish a falcon hospital under her tutelage. Her presence had proved to be a godsend. It was she that had distributed free suture packs to the local falconers, thereby eliminating the risk of eye infections caused by dirty needles and thread. Suppressing his apprehension, he slipped his left hand into the protective cuff, coaxed the falcon onto it, steeled himself, and walked in.

He was immediately struck by the dramatic change in temperature. He had heard of air conditioning, but now he felt its magic for the first time. He stood alone before an unmanned reception desk in the entry vestibule, disoriented, awkward, needing to announce his presence but unsure how to do so. On a whim, he reached back to the open door and slammed it shut.

The doctor and veterinary technician team of Jane Lambert and Uzair Jangi were evaluating fecal, crop and blood samples taken from a male Arctic Peregrine falcon, part of a routine pre-purchase examination commissioned by the palace, when they were startled by the thud of the front door. Jane glanced up from her microscope. "Please see who that is, Uzi," she said to her assistant.

As Uzi slid off his stool and disappeared into the anteroom, Jane reflected with pleasure on how quickly he had become an indispensable part of the operation.

She had run it alone for the first two months, because there simply wasn't anyone else around with the training to be a useful aide. Then the Emir had sent word to his emissaries in Asia, and the one in Pakistan had answered the call. In the four months since his arrival, Uzi—as he had asked to be called—had proven to be an excellent recruit. At thirty-six, with a wife and daughter back in Pakistan who would be allowed to join him upon renewal of his one-year contract, his professionalism was underpinned by a passion for his work. In a mutually beneficial arrangement, a couple of patient rooms at one end of the old hospital had been converted into makeshift living quarters for Uzi, who was only too happy to live rent-free and not have to drive to work. Jane appreciated him being on the premises around the clock, as some of the local falconers were not pre-disposed to limiting their visits to official hours. She was just as grateful for Uzi's passable command of the Arabic language, which he had studied specifically with an eye to the salaries the oil-rich Gulf states had garnered a reputation for. She had started to learn the language herself right after she had married Zaig, but that remained a work in progress. Having Uzi to practice with at the hospital was a bonus, not least for how he facilitated communication with the clients, most of whom didn't speak English. She had barely turned her eye back to the microscope when she heard him call out to her with a trill of urgency.

"Doctor Lambert! Come please!"

The man she found Uzi with was obviously a local, for he wore a white *thobe,* the flowing white cotton tunic that was standard garb for men in the Gulf, with a red and white *ghutra* head-cloth covering his hair. He had a mustache that Jane thought might be purposed to make him look older. Low to mid-twenties, she guessed. Handsome, but his expression betrayed insecurity. He regarded her nervously, averted his eyes at first, then he thrust his left arm out towards her and she saw what had gotten Uzi excited.

"Well, well," she murmured, stepping closer. "What have we here?"

"He trapped it this morning," Uzi said with wide-eyed wonder.

"Did he now!" Jane took in the charcoal grey plumage. "This is a rare sight indeed!"

"It looks like a mix, no?" Uzi said. "Maybe Gyrfalcon and Saker? See, it has two broken wings."

Jane nodded as he pointed them out.

"Let's imp them right away." She beckoned to the man and said in Arabic, "Come."

With her focus on the splendor of the falcon, Jane hadn't noticed the man's fixation on her. She was dressed in modestly loose-fitting surgical scrubs, the top extending down below her hips to hide her figure, yet he was mesmerized. The combination of pearl white skin, shoulder-length black hair tied back in a little ponytail, and the first set of blue eyes he had ever seen, left him breathless. The circle of unveiled women he had ever stood this close to was his mother, one aunt, a female cousin, and the neighbor's daughter that had set his heart aflutter. This woman was something else. Blue eyes! They were kind eyes, comforting eyes, and he felt relief. Not only was she physically striking, but in addition to being a bird doctor, she also spoke to him in Arabic!

He followed her to a room in which six hooded falcons perched a foot off the white-tiled floor atop three padded benches. He had never seen so many falcons in one place at one time, but then he had learned to trap and train from his father, who had only ever owned three birds. He recognized these six as Sakers, favored throughout the gulf for being versatile hunters of the Houbara, Arabian falconers' preferred prey. Pristine specimens, but, he noted with relish, all smaller than his, and not as rare. Uzi noticed him eyeing them.

"They are palace falcons," said Uzi, straightening his posture. He added with a gratuitous whisper, "They belong to the Emir!"

The man wasn't sure if Uzi was trying to impress him or warn him off touching them, but the effect was both. His falcon in the same room as those of the Emir! Maybe he was out of place, but his falcon certainly wasn't!

A single shelf ran at hip height around the room, bearing a number of red and blue open-top plastic boxes containing cotton wool, bandages, syringes and other assorted medical paraphernalia. But the focal point of the room was a stainless-steel examination table, to which Jane wheeled a stool. She tapped the top of the table with an open palm. The man reluctantly deposited on it his prized possession. Jane reached for a black rubber tube coiled around the top of a metal canister lined against the wall next to the table. A transparent plastic cone adorned its end. After Uzi eased the cone over the falcon's head, Jane turned a lever on the canister. A hiss announced the flow of gas, and the falcon went limp.

Jane opened a flat drawer containing a large selection of wing and tail feathers. She sampled a few against the falcon's wing and settled on two. She cut the broken feathers cleanly above the break. Then she measured one of the replacement feathers against each cut one and snipped it in turn to the length that exactly matched the missing part of each broken feather.

The man watched with the intensity of someone witnessing his newborn baby undergoing open-heart surgery.

Jane dabbed epoxy glue onto two bamboo pegs and inserted them into the hollow shafts of the replacement feathers, leaving half an inch of the pegs exposed. She added more glue to the protruding section of the pegs and gingerly inserted them into the hollow shafts of the broken feathers. The lengths matched perfectly. Before the glue had a chance to set, she rotated the replacement sections to line up with the originals, and she was done. Uzi touched up her handiwork over the joints, making the repairs virtually invisible to the naked eye. The falcon's feathers now restored, Jane turned the gas off. Within minutes, the bird awoke.

The man's delight was tempered when he was informed they would keep their newest patient overnight to give the glue additional time to set. Jane, now a veritable Goddess in his eyes, opened a textbook and displayed color photographs of an identical raptor.

"It's a female Altai Saker," she said. "Falco Cherrug Altaicus." She turned the page to a map. "From the Altai mountains in Asia, where Russia, China, Mongolia and Kazakhstan come together."

"*Sinjari?*" The man asked.

"Yes, *Sinjari,*" Uzi said. "Altai Saker."

"Altai…Sa…"

"Saker. Altai Saker."

The man smiled. "*Al-tayr*…Altai."

Jane appreciated his wit. She was familiar enough with the language to know *Al-tayr* was Arabic for "the bird."

"What's your name?" she asked in the same tongue.

"Salman Shahab."

Uzi jotted it down on a form. "Your address?" he asked.

Salman gestured with his hand towards the window. "Magwa."

The irony gave Jane pause. Within the confines of the room were falcons from the extremes of the social landscape, the emiri palace and Magwa. How fascinating that the six representing the elite were outclassed by the one from the bottom rung.

"I will take it," Salman said, pointing to his falcon.

"Do not worry," Uzi replied. "I live here, in the hospital. It is safe. You can take it in the morning."

Salman looked like he wanted to argue, but reluctantly conceded. "Please, don't feed it," he said.

Uzi glanced at Jane, who nodded.

"We won't," Uzi said.

"Till the morning," Salman said, a glint in his eye. He walked towards the door. Before leaving, he stopped and looked back, first at the falcon, then at Jane, his joy irrepressible. "Altai!" he said.

"Altai," Jane replied with a smile.

Chapter Two

Of the three men who presented themselves at the falcon hospital the next morning, two were expected, the third a surprise. First through the doors was Rashed, the palace falcon handler, there to pick up the emiri six. After learning that Jane had deemed them all hale, he might have been on his way sooner but for the riveting glimpse he caught of the Altai.

"*Sinjari!*"

In over thirty years of service as falcon handler for the incumbent Emir and the prior one, he had known only one such raptor, during a brief stint in 1958, before it had proven too independent and flown off during a session late in the training regimen. Now he admired the breathtaking splendor of this paragon, inquired as to its provenance and ownership, and hustled out, eager to inform his master. As he drove off towards the road, he had no way of knowing that the young man who passed him in a pickup truck going in the opposite direction was the paragon's own master.

Salman noted that the Toyota Land Cruiser leaving the hospital bore the distinctive license plates of the palace fleet, and he wondered if whoever was driving it had laid eyes on his *Sinjari*. He hoped so. The thought gave him a bizarre thrill, laced as it was with the threat of the unknown. He dared not imagine what might ensue if the Emir learned that there was one falcon in the land superior to all of his.

He found Dr. Lambert focusing the lens of an Asahi Pentax 35mm single-lens-reflex camera on his hawk. The flash alarmed him, until she assured him it was harmless. He watched as Jane fired off a succession of frames from different angles, then took turns with Uzi as they photographed each other with the raptor. As he was leaving, Jane accompanied him outside and snapped more shots in the natural light, now of a proud Salman with his falcon.

It was two hours later, with Salman long gone, that Uzi heard the day's third visitor before he saw him. A distant rumble grew to a deep-toned growl as a streak of bright yellow zipped past the window. Uzi jumped up from the reception desk and peered out at a gleaming Corvette Sting Ray, the most outrageous muscle car he had ever beheld. The man who emerged from behind the tinted glass wore a white tee shirt and faded denim jeans over black leather cowboy boots. Black hair hung to his shoulders, and even with his gold-rimmed Ray-Ban aviator sunglasses, Uzi instantly recognized him. Jane also heard the bassy notes of the 360HP V8, and her curiosity brought her next to Uzi at the window.

"Prince Bader," Uzi whispered excitedly, "Son of the Emir!" They stepped back as Prince Bader entered.

"Good morning, your excellency!" Uzi said deferentially, eager to show that he knew whose company he was in.

Prince Bader ignored him and extended his right hand out to Jane.

"You must be Dr. Lambert. I've heard about you from my father."

The initial impression Jane had of him was that he purposely rolled his Rs to sound American. Rather than impressing her, it had the opposite effect.

"Pleased to meet you," she replied, noting he had not removed his sunglasses. Was that insecurity? More ersatz cool?

"I am told you have a special falcon in your care."

"You must be talking about the Altai Saker. No longer with us, I'm afraid."

"No?" His displeasure was immediately evident.

"It's back with its owner."

"Who is the owner?" His tone was distinctly authoritative, as if warning her against not telling him.

"Salman Shahab."

"Do you know where he lives?"

"In Magwa."

"Hm." The sound of the boot-heels added to the prince's imposing demeanor as he walked to the reception desk and reached for the telephone. He turned the rotary dial from memory, demanded an immediate call back with whatever details were on file for Salman Shahab, dictated the number registered on the dial, and plopped the handset back on the cradle. He removed his sunglasses and turned to Jane.

"The first falcon hospital. My father is a real visionary. Come on, show me around."

Jane got the distinct impression he was not asking her but telling her.

The return call came within minutes. Uzi laid the handset on the desk and scuttled off to find them in the room where Jane had imped the Altai's feathers. They were hunched over the same textbook Jane had pulled off a shelf the day before, open to the same photographs of an Altai Saker falcon.

"Telephone for your excellency."

Prince Bader abruptly broke away from Jane's side and brushed past Uzi.

"Don't let him bother you," Jane whispered to Uzi.

They followed Prince Bader back to the reception, where he picked up the phone with an air of impatience. The news he received left him visibly exasperated. Jane was too wary to inquire, but she didn't have to.

"There is no record of any Salman Shahab," Prince Bader said after he hung up. "He must be *Bidoon*." He sighed irritably. "If he comes back here before I find him, tell him I want to see the

Sinjari. Have him leave it here, and call Rashed at the palace." With that, and without once acknowledging Uzi's presence, he walked out.

Uzi tried to hide the pain of the disdain but Jane could see the humiliation in his eyes. She put a comforting hand on his shoulder and he knew that she knew.

"It's all right," she said. "It reflects less on you than it does on him."

Uzi nodded.

"What is *Bidoon?*" Jane asked.

Uzi shrugged. "Maybe he meant bedouin."

"He said *Bidoon*."

"*Bidoon* means without."

Jane's expression turned quizzical. "Without what?"

Again Uzi shrugged. "Just ... without."

***

Prince Bader drove around the side of the hospital and stopped. It was a good vantage point overlooking the shacks of Magwa. He shifted the gear to neutral and left the engine in idle so the air conditioner would keep him cool. He took two cigarettes from a pack on the passenger seat, lit one and tore open the other, spilling the tobacco into the concave cavity of a half oyster shell. He retrieved a small leather pouch from the glove compartment, unzipped it, and took out a block of concentrated reddish-brown resin. He broke off a little piece and held it with tweezers just above the flame of his lighter, until its smoke permeated the car with what he considered the world's most enticing aroma. He mixed it into the tobacco and rolled the mixture in a sheet of cigarette paper. He lit it and inhaled deeply, thinking that tinted car windows were a great invention. Not that he worried about anyone seeing him, far from it. Indeed, the only awkwardness would arise if his father found out, but no one else would dare say a word. The old man was already grumpy enough about the poor grades he had graduated with from the University of Southern California, about his long hair and his preference for wearing western jeans instead of the ubiquitous local *thobe*.

The familiar sensation spread throughout his body, and a euphoric haze permeated his mind. Now he could think straight.

He rationalized that it was a generational thing. The old man had never been to university, let alone one in California. He was from a legacy school of thought that believed university was all about courses and classes and credits. He had no inkling of the extra-curricular activities on a liberal American campus, of the variety of lures that appealed to a contemporary man's hedonistic bent. The challenge now was to impress him, to recapture the warm and fuzzy—those Americans had some great expressions—that existed between them before father had shipped son off to be molded by a western education into something he didn't want to be.

The old man's birthday was ten days hence, and Bader had grappled with the dilemma of what he could gift the man who had everything. Until that morning, when he'd heard from Rashed about the *Sinjari*. He had immediately told Rashed to say nothing to his father. The man who had everything was a falconry aficionado; he had Peregrines and Sakers and Barbaries, but he didn't have a *Sinjari*.

He peered contemptuously down at the shacks of Magwa. Somewhere down in that slum there was a hawk that had been described as a *Sinjari* of unprecedented beauty.

Dilemma solved.

He took one last toke of the joint and flicked it out the window. He wasn't about to wade into that cesspool, but then he didn't have to. He was accustomed to commanding others to do the dirty work.

He would task the police with finding Salman Shahab, and find him they most certainly would.

***

Magnificent as she was, Salman knew he would only prove he was worthy of her if he succeeded in training her and she deferred only to him. The concept had fascinated him at an early age, how his desert-roaming forebears had supplemented their diet with meat attained by first trapping wild falcons, then training the raptors to hunt for them. In times past it had been a matter of sustenance. Now it was sport, one in which the price of participation was luck, patience and skill. He had made an auspicious start, for luck had bequeathed to him a rare empress. He had the discipline to be patient, but the skill factor was yet to be proven. This would be his debut solo training session, and he was eager to apply what he had learned from his father. He intended to keep things simple and nail the fundamentals. "There is a delicate balance to be maintained," he said, "a tug of wills to be finessed."

Hamza soaked it up, grateful that Salman had let him tag along.

They were at a secluded spot beyond the edge of Magwa, behind a dune where Salman could command the falcon's attention without distractions. She was motionless, standing comfortably flat-footed atop the padded round surface of a *wakir,* a portable hardwood mushroom-shaped perch anchored in the ground. She saw nothing; her eyelids were held closed by the thread tied above her head, effectively blocking the light from reaching her pupils, naturally tranquilizing her into a near-hypnotic, manageable state.

Salman admired her spotted crop. Such a dazzling bird, big and strong, reputedly an aggressive, no-holds-barred hunter. Not as fast as a Peregrine, but said to possess superior stamina. More the tactical hunter, ideally suited to the taxing physical demands of chasing Houbara. His request that she not be fed during her overnight stay at the hospital had been well-founded, as hunger would initially mellow her wildness, important at the onset of training.

He stroked her claws with a small strip of fresh pigeon meat. She bit, but didn't try to eat. He pulled the meat away.

"Altai!"

He stepped back and paced around her in an arc.

"Altai!" He repeated it slowly, distinctly, like a mantra.

Her primary stimulus was visual, so even though she heard him, her closed eyelids prevented her from seeing him. He came back and touched her talons again with the meat. "Altai!"

He repeated the cycle, awaiting the first sign that she was accepting of her new reality. It was subtle when it came, a less aggressive bite, after which she allowed the meat to dwell long enough in her beak to taste it.

"Altai!"

He pulled the meat back, instinct telling him to keep her fasting one more day. She had already started to lose weight; by tomorrow, hunger pangs would make her more receptive. Simple fundamentals.

"Tomorrow, she will eat," he said to Hamza.

"How do you know?"

"Tomorrow you will see."

***

Wadha Shahab was kneading a preserve of parched flour, dried dates and *samn,* the clarified butter that was a staple of the local diet, when the sound of the Datsun heralded her son's arrival. She looked up as he pulled aside the canvas door curtain.

"See, mother," Salman said, "Here it is!"

Wadha couldn't tell one falcon from another, but she indulged her son. "Truly, you did not exaggerate her beauty. Your father will be impressed. Are you going to get him?"

Salman beamed at her. Without her black *abaya* covering her head, she was exposed like she would never be outside the shack. To his eyes, she, too, was beautiful, albeit through her perpetual mask of resignation. Even now her labored smile made her appear a decade older than her thirty-five years.

"I will go now. First, I wanted to ask you, can it sleep inside?"

"Please, no! There is barely enough room for the three of us."

"Then I will sleep outside with it."

"As you wish. The situation will improve after we move. Your father says the new town will be ready by the end of the year." Wadha turned back to the task at hand. "May Allah bless the government for building us new, permanent homes."

"Bless them?" Salman sneered. "They are not building a new town out of concern for us, they are doing it because every foreigner that arrives at the airport has to pass through the middle of Magwa on the way to Ahmadi, and it is an embarrassment for the Emir and his crony ministers. If the sons of whores cared about us, they would give us what they give everyone else, education, healthcare, benefits. But for us, nothing. They don't even allow us to drive on the roads! Sons of whores!"

"Keep your voice down!" his mother pleaded. "You know I don't like to hear you say these things. We don't want trouble."

"Allah has blessed them enough! Go see the palaces they build for themselves!"

"I beg of you, don't talk like this. It will only bring you harm. Our lot in life is Allah's will. Promise me!"

Salman eyed her indignantly. "Is it Allah's will that one family owns the country? Or is it because in prior generations they were more ruthless than the other clans? Is it Allah's will that we should be deprived while they live in excess? Our lot is what we allow it to be. You and father and everyone else around here are too docile. I will not accept a life of shit!" He nodded defiantly, turned, and walked out of the shack.

As was her instinct every time it happened, Wadha Shahab murmured prayers for her son as she watched him go.

Salman took the desert road for the few miles to the tank farm, ever aware that being caught driving on a paved road meant certain arrest. At nineteen he was too young anyway to apply for a driver license, but his age was not the issue. Even when he turned twenty-one, his status, or more accurately lack thereof, disqualified him from applying for any official documentation.

The construction site came into view within minutes. It seemed that they were erecting a new storage tank every week, and he could now count thirteen of the twenty his father said would be built. The transformation of the desert was an amazing sight to behold. Salman hoped his father would continue to be employed there after construction was complete. The old man was optimistic, for the tank farm would be owned and operated by the oil company, so it wasn't the government. At least not yet.

Faisal Shahab was waiting inside the guardhouse, standing vigil at the window, eager to see the falcon his son had raved about. As the Datsun approached, he stepped outside and waved. Salman waved back and honked. He always found it amusing how awkward and uncomfortable his father looked in the oversized green khaki guard uniform.

Salman stepped out of the pickup truck with the falcon on his wrist.

"Allaaaaah!" Faisal crooned. "Truly the most magnificent hawk I have seen! Be proud, my son! Congratulations!"

"Look, you can't even tell any of the feathers have been replaced!"

"It is true! That doctor is a magician!"

"It didn't eat this morning. Allah willing, it will eat tomorrow."

"Don't worry, it will eat. Truly, it is bigger than we have seen! Let's go home so I can change, then we will get it a new *burqa*, for the ones we have will be too tight for its head!"

***

As they routinely did on Curry Tuesdays, Dr. Abdul-Razzaq "Zaig" Yassine and his wife met for lunch at the Hubara Club, the social and sports facility exclusive to Kuwait Oil Company staff beyond a certain employment grade. Zaig and Jane made it a point to get there early, for the Indian chefs were masters of their craft, and the dining room always filled to capacity. They sat at a perimeter table, next to a wall of glass. As he peered out at the bikini-clad teenagers frolicking in the swimming pool, Zaig reflected on how Ahmadi was an oasis of liberalism in a land of taboos. It was the price the country had to pay to reap the riches of the black gold it floated on, a resource that could not be harvested without the expertise of foreigners that had lifestyle requirements so at odds with the native cultural underpinnings. The expertise came courtesy of a joint venture between the Anglo-Persian oil company, precursor of British Petroleum, and Gulf Oil, the two companies that had won Kuwait's oil concession rights in 1934. Three decades on from that seminal event, Zaig was proud to be one of the handful of Kuwaitis who had merited a position of prestige at KOC. He was confident it would be no more than another decade, at most, before Kuwait assumed ownership of the company, and the pendulum of staff nationalities swung in favor of the locals. In the meantime, he would relish the sight of the scantily-clad westerners while he could. The westerner he loved and had married waited until their orders were taken before surprising him with a question.

"What is *Bidoon?*"

Zaig arched an eyebrow at Jane. "Where did that come from?"

"Remember I told you about the Altai falcon that was brought to the hospital yesterday?"

"The one with the broken feathers?"

"Yes. The Emir's falcon handler saw it this morning when he came to pick up the palace falcons. Next thing you know the Emir's son shows up in his fancy American sports car demanding to see it."

"Prince Bader?"

"Yes. All full of himself, I must say. Acted very snottily towards Uzi. Anyway, by then the young lad who trapped the Altai had already come in and taken it. Prince Bader demanded his name, and I couldn't not tell him. He telephoned someone and wasn't half displeased when they couldn't find any official record of Salman Shahab. That's when he said Salman Shahab is likely *Bidoon*. What's *Bidoon?*"

Zaig lowered his voice. "*Bidoon* is short for *Bidoon jinsiyyah*. The literal translation is without citizenship." He cleared his throat without having to, an impulse Jane recognized as a sign of discomfort. She let his words hang for a moment.

"So Salman Shahab is not a Kuwaiti citizen?"

An English couple were shown to the adjacent table. After the requisite exchange of pleasantries, Zaig winked at Jane.

"What?" she said.

"Later."

***

Jane broached the subject again that evening, when they were alone in their air-conditioned prefab bungalow, against the melodic strains of *Rubber Soul* on the turntable. "If Salman's not Kuwaiti, what is he?"

Zaig shot back a *do-we-have-to-talk-about-this?* expression. When Jane made it clear that they did, he sighed. He reached for the amplifier's volume knob, then changed his mind. Jane wondered whether he had thought of lowering the volume or raising it.

"Kuwait achieved independence in 1961, just seven years ago. Before independence, and in preparation for it, the government started a process to register all Kuwaitis. In 1959 a law was enacted that established parameters for citizenship. Basically, people had to prove that they had been residents of Kuwait since 1920. That was easy for the merchant class, people like my parents, and those who were known around the population centers, especially those on the coast. But for some, particularly the inland bedouins, it was not so easy. Some of them didn't have any proof, others simply weren't even aware what was happening, or if they heard about it, it was such an alien concept to them and their way of life that they dismissed it as unnecessary. Since independence, only citizens are beneficiaries of the government-sponsored improvements in the standard of living that oil has enabled. Those who didn't register are…not citizens."

Jane took a moment to absorb what she'd heard.

"So they are disenfranchised," she surmised.

"Well…it depends who you ask."

"What do you think?"

Zaig frowned. "I don't. It's not my problem."

"So are all of the people in Magwa *Bidoons?*"

"I don't know," Zaid replied, a hint of irritation in his tone. "I'm sure some of them are. Regardless, the government is building them a new town. Magwa has to go. The only way to do that is to move the people who live there, and you need somewhere to move them to, and it has to be somewhere better. Otherwise they will resist."

Jane thought about Salman. She saw him in a different light now, one that better illuminated what had come across as a vague persona. Was what she had perceived as reticence perhaps a mask for vulnerability? She was suddenly filled with empathy.

"But if they don't have citizenship…" Jane tried to decipher the ramifications.

"It's not our problem."

"I know. I'm just trying to understand the extent of the problem. Not from our perspective, or…or the government's, but from theirs."

"Why?"

"Well, for starters because I've never heard of anything like it."

"Of course you have," Zaig retorted. "Europe has its gypsies."

Jane looked at him pensively.

Zaig reached over and squeezed her arm. "Why are you so interested in the *Bidoon?*"

"Because there was something disparaging about the way Prince Bader called Salman a *Bidoon.*"

"Leave it alone, darling." Zaig glanced at his watch. "Come on, let's go to bed." He lifted the arm off the vinyl album and turned off the turntable and amplifier.

Jane mulled over the concept of national independence and the parameters countries set for citizenship at the time of independence. There was no standard universal formula that she was aware of, but then it wasn't a subject she had ever pondered before. She tried to dismiss it, but there was something she couldn't articulate that simmered in her consciousness, a nag she couldn't shake. Then it occurred to her that the gypsies in Europe roamed around freely from one country to another, and those who ended up in the UK didn't just paddle across the English Channel and saunter up a British beach. They had to be processed through the UK border agency, and for that they had to have passports, which meant they had to be citizens of some country or another. Didn't they?

She decided not to push the subject further with Zaig. It was clear he wasn't comfortable talking about it. Plus, he was right. It wasn't their problem.

Chapter Three

Salman slept on a rug outdoors, within touching distance of the *wakir* and the falcon that graced it like a royal on a throne, under a sky lit by a full moon that anchored a remarkable sprinkling of astral glitter. Even his mother had commented that it was as if the eyes of the heavens were gazing down upon them. His sleep was fitful, like the first night with a new love so consuming he had to keep raising his head at her silhouette to confirm she wasn't a dream.

A light breeze wafted in at dawn from over the gulf, ruffling the scrubby Zygophyllum bushes that dotted the sandy hillocks east of town. He sat up, energized by the knowledge that his days were now spiced with a new flavor. As he rose, he discerned a movement to his left and sensed he was not alone.

"Who is there?"

"It is me," Hamza replied. The neighbors' son stood up from his squat.

"Why are you out so early?"

"I don't want you to leave without me."

Salman couldn't fault the boy's enthusiasm. He had known him from practically the day he was born, thirteen years ago, and he knew Hamza regarded him as an older brother. Salman hoped he would one day be his brother-in-law.

"Go tell your parents you will be with me."

"They know, I told them yesterday."

The training spot was a mere ten-minute walk from Magwa, yet suitably isolated. The sun had not yet peeked over the horizon when they reached it.

Salman had learned from his father that it wasn't cruel to withhold food from a falcon, as long as it was done in the right measure. Not only was it not cruel, it was natural. Why, his father had stressed, it was what adult falcons did to their fledglings to goad them to leave the nest so they could learn to hunt for themselves. It was the first thing Salman taught Hamza. The second was the importance of giving a new falcon a name and using it.

"Altai!"

She was already beginning to recognize his voice. Her eyelids had begun to sag against the thread, allowing through enough light to produce faint peripheral images. Now when he moved around her she was visually aware of it. But her overbearing sense today was hunger. The feel of the meat brushing against her toes was less of an annoyance. This time she knew what it was, and she wanted more than a taste. Salman knowingly prodded her with a morsel; she bit, and she swallowed.

Salman smiled and stroked her breast with a pigeon feather, then fed her another bite.

"See?" he said to Hamza.

The boy beamed.

"The trick is to give it enough to preclude it getting too weak, but not enough to sate its hunger." It was a fine balance, when to give and when to withhold, one for which a trainer's instinct could only be honed by experience.

He had fitted her with a brand new *subuq,* jesses consisting of braided nylon-cord tethers connected on one side to leather cuffs strapped around each ankle, and on the other to a single-cord leash tied to the shaft of the *wakir* on which she was perched, to preclude her taking flight when her vision was restored. The leash was adorned mid-length by a steel swivel that prevented it from twisting and coiling around itself.

"Pay attention, Hamza. It is time to introduce it to the single most important accessory in falconry."

"The *burqa!*" Hamza guessed.

Salman reached into the pocket of his *thobe* and retrieved the leather hood his father had purchased the day before at a market stall in the city. It was sized to fit snugly enough to prevent the entry of light, essentially blindfolding her, while bulbing around her eyes to avoid contact. Not so much now, but in the next few days, when her eyelids sagged enough to expose her pupils, at which time the hood would become her tranquilizer. But first, she had to learn to accept it.

He positioned himself to her side. The hood was in his right hand, the little decorative leather plume on its head between his index and middle fingers. The opening for the beak faced his thumb. She was not aware what was happening, what little vision she had being strictly peripheral. He placed the chin-strap that separated the beak opening from the neck space just beneath her mandible, and deftly rolled the hood onto her head. He left it there a few seconds, then slipped it off.

For almost an hour, Hamza watched as Salman repeated the cycle, patiently, each time leaving it on her for a little while longer, letting her get accustomed to it in spurts, until she was accepting of it for several minutes at a time. That was measurable success at this stage, and too much too soon ran the risk of backfiring, so he ended the session in order to preserve and consolidate the progress they had made.

As they walked home, Hamza told Salman that the training session was the best time he had ever had. Salman agreed. How sharply that good time contrasted with the drudgery of what awaited him now, the slog of his daily job search. Ripe and able-bodied as he was, in days of yore he would have headed to the coast and found an apprenticeship in the pearl diving trade. That way of life had disappeared, sidelined by the new paradigm. The oil industry had ushered in a construction and development boom, but it was off limits to his ilk, not just illiterate and bereft of any commercial skills, but lacking even the most basic of foundational markers, an identity card. He was now of an age where he understood his predicament. Going to school was not an option, for the schools were government-run, and the government didn't want to educate him. He could recite Koranic verses, at least those his parents had taught him, but they had taught him the way they had learned, by rote. He was prepared to start with the alphabet, but even for that, he needed someone to learn from. He knew no one who could read, let alone teach. He knew how to trap a falcon, and he believed he knew how to train it to hunt for him, but how could that be parlayed into sustainable income? Who employed falconers? The ruling class. Even if there were openings, which there weren't, Salman wouldn't countenance working for the establishment he so despised, for they were the cause of the misery. In time, Hamza would come to learn all this, if he hadn't already.

On the approach to Magwa, they attracted the attention of a scrum of children who ran to them, drawn to the spectacle perched on Salman's wrist. Giddy with excitement, they reaffirmed what Salman already knew, that with this falcon, he was a man transformed.

A short while later it was the same group of children who ran to the shack and alerted Salman that he was the subject of a police search. Alarmed, Wadha Shahab beseeched her son to be respectful as the two of them stepped outside in time for the approach of a dark grey Jeep behind a running boy. The boy stopped and pointed.

"In the name of Allah, what have you done?" Wadha demanded from behind the veil of her *abaya*.

"By Allah, nothing!" Salman replied, his voice tinged with dread of the humiliation that any encounter with the authorities could bring. Hamza emerged from the shack next door, followed by his sister. If there was to be humiliation, Salman thought, more than anything else he did not want Hissa to see it.

A policeman in an oversized uniform emerged from the front passenger seat when the Jeep pulled up. "Where is Salman Shahab?" he said gruffly.

"Why?" Salman said.

"You answer, you do not ask." The policeman eyed the falcon on the *wakir* next to the shack before turning again to Salman. "Are you Salman Shahab?"

"Yes."

"Bring the *Sinjari* and come with us."

"Where?"

"I said you don't ask."

"May Allah prolong your life," Wadha pleaded, "where are you taking my son?"

"You stay here. He will be back soon."

Salman sat in the back of the Jeep, the falcon on his arm, the two policemen in the front. Hamza took off running behind the Jeep, urged by Hissa to see if he could find out where they were taking Salman.

It was a short ride to the crest of the ridge, where a yellow Corvette was waiting in front of the hospital. The guttural rumble of its idling engine sounded intimidating to Salman, like the deep growl of a menacing dog.

"Down!" the policeman ordered.

Salman found himself face-to-face with Prince Bader, now dressed in a white *thobe* and a beige *bisht*, the flowing outer cloak that imparted prestige and stature. On his head was a white *ghutra* held in place by a black *agal*. The only constant from his appearance at the hospital the day before were the sunglasses. The overall effect was one of unmistakable power and authority.

"Peace be upon you," Prince Bader said amiably.

"And upon you, peace." Salman's reply was spontaneous, far from heartfelt.

"Nice *Sinjari.*"

Salman didn't react. That this was about the Altai was clear from the moment the police told him to bring it with him.

"How did you acquire it?"

"I trapped it."

"Allah has bestowed upon you great luck. First he blesses you with a *Sinjari*, then sends you a buyer to whom you can sell it for good—"

"It is not for sale."

"—money." The prince tilted his head. "What did you say?"

"The *Sinjari* is not for sale."

Salman couldn't see Prince Bader's eyes, but he could feel them pierce him.

Prince Bader's face slowly registered bemusement. "That cannot be. Everything is for sale. The only question is the price."

Salman's heart was thumping, but his demeanor was as impassive as that of the falcon.

"One hundred dinars," the prince offered.

By Salman's standards, a lot of money, but he remained unmoved.

Prince Bader reached into his pocket and pulled out a wad of cash. "Three hundred." He licked a thumb and started to count banknotes.

Salman's eyes flicked down to the money, more than he had ever seen. The notes the prince held out to him barely put a dent in the pile. The policeman watching the exchange shuffled his feet.

Salman didn't react.

"By Allah, you drive a hard bargain," Prince Bader said. He extracted several more banknotes. "I will let you get the better of me. Five hundred."

With his back to the road, Salman didn't see the approaching Wolseley, but Prince Bader did, and he was none the happier for it. Jane's car lacked air-conditioning, so her windows were down. The look of surprise was evident on her face as she pulled up next to the Corvette, the police Jeep and the three men standing in between them.

"Hallo," she said cheerily. She cut the engine and stepped down from the car. "I see you've met the Altai!"

"Indeed," Prince Bader replied. Jane had spoken in English, so he was the only man there who understood her words.

"Quite the beauty, isn't she?"

"Truly."

Jane sensed from Prince Bader's terse responses that she might be interrupting something.

"Is everything alright?" she asked. She looked at Salman and said in Arabic, "*Kul shay tamam?*"

It was Prince Bader who replied.

"Very impressive, Dr. Lambert. Yes, all is fine. We are just conducting a little business to give this falcon a home and care worthy of its stature. You may continue to your work. All is well here."

Instinct told her otherwise, but she was not about to challenge him. "Right! Well then, I'll be off." Her eyes were on the rearview mirror as she left them and repaired to the hospital.

Prince Bader guessed she would be watching, a typically inquisitive and meddlesome woman. He turned back to Salman. "I am a busy man," he said, irritation tweaking his tone. "I respect your need to think about your price, so I will return at the same time tomorrow and we will conclude this transaction in the manner that you are happy with. I know you will be reasonable."

Salman was relieved this episode was ending, so he said nothing lest he prolong it. Prince Bader gestured once to the policeman with his head, then got into his car and drove off towards the road. The Jeep followed him. It was not lost on Salman that they didn't bother to take him back home. He spat on the ground and started walking.

"Salman!"

He turned around and saw Uzi running towards him.

"Salman!" the Pakistani was panting when he caught up to him. "Please! Bring the falcon so the doctor can check the feathers!"

The feathers were fine, and Salman knew it. But he was still rattled by the encounter with the royal, and he had a sense the doctor's appearance had worked in his favor, even if he didn't know quite how. Now he could see her standing outside the hospital, watching them. There was something reassuring about her. He went along. Out of the shadows of Magwa, the lone figure of Hamza appeared, running towards the hospital. As Salman and Uzi approached, Jane held the door open for them. Together with Uzi, they ushered Salman into the same room where Jane had imped the falcon's feathers.

"Ask him what was going on out there," Jane said to Uzi.

Through the ensuing three-way conversation, translated in both directions by Uzi, Jane learned first the gist, then the details, scant though they were. She asked if Salman planned to sell. With a shake of his head he expressed his desire not to. She probed as to whether he thought he could resist the persuasion of an insistent Prince Bader, financial and otherwise. That was when a look of uncertainty washed over Salman's face, when his vulnerability became palpable.

"Tell him I think he needs to set a high price, but not so high that it might be perceived as insulting."

After listening to Uzi, Salman looked at her with searching eyes. "How much?" he said.

Jane was lost for a number.

"I would say more than has ever been paid for a falcon by anyone in the country. That would be justified because this is such a rare bird. Young, female, healthy. Should make a great hunter."

Salman was deep in thought. Jane expected him to say he had no idea what the standing record price for a falcon was in these parts, but he didn't. He asked for information, but gave away not a hint of how he was processing it. It occurred to her those were traits of a good negotiator. Yet she felt he was out of his depth, considering who was on the other side of the table. Inexplicably, she also felt protective of him.

"Tell him I think he is going to have to sell. I will inquire about the highest price that has been paid for a falcon. That will give us a benchmark."

Salman's response was terse. "The prince will come back tomorrow morning."

Jane pursed her lips. "Let him show you where he lives so we know how to find him," she said to Uzi. "Go! *Yalla!*"

As the three of them made their way to the door, Salman realized that the doctor hadn't checked his falcon's feathers. He realized she had never intended to. Before he stepped outside he turned to her and uttered a word of thanks. The parting smile he received in return was heartfelt, and with it she masked her apprehension. She watched as Salman, now accompanied by Uzi and a boy who had waited outside the door, headed back to Magwa.

***

It is not for sale.

Prince Bader chuckled disdainfully as he thought about the *Bidoon* boy's attitude. But it was to be expected, not unusual for a seller's opening position in a negotiation started by an interested buyer. He had to give it to the kid, although he was sure that by now the falcon would have changed hands, but for the ill-timed intervention of the English doctor.

Everything is for sale; the only question is the price.

A universal truth. He wondered what the price might be for the English doctor. Not bad-looking, that one. Too bad she was married to a Kuwaiti. Had her husband been one of her own kind, there may have been possibilities for some naughtiness. Alas, she was not only married to a local, but one of considerable renown.

A thousand dinars, that's what Salman Shahab will want for the falcon. The boy probably couldn't even count that high, but no problem. At that price that bird was a steal. Indeed, the higher the price, the more appropriate a birthday present for his father. The only aggravation was the need to drive back out to Magwa tomorrow to do the deal. And do the deal tomorrow he would, for there was a limit to his patience. A good negotiation was always fun as long as it didn't cross the line to disrespect. The *Bidoon* boy wouldn't dare. If he did, he'd have to be taught a lesson. Come to think of it, that, too, would be fun.

Prince Bader was pleased with himself. This was a win-win situation. Life was good. He pulled a vial out of the glove compartment, unscrewed the cap, and eyed the white powder. Life was very good. His left hand controlled the steering wheel, the vial between the thumb and forefinger, as his right hand fished a tiny silver spoon out of his breast pocket. He glanced at the rearview mirror, dipped the spoon in the vial and filled it. He jammed the top of his knees against the steering wheel, blocked a nostril with a finger, and snorted the contents of the spoon. The shot of euphoria was instantaneous. He dipped the spoon again, switched nostrils, and took another snort. A bump in the road jarred him and his knees lost control of the steering wheel. He grabbed it with his hands, and in the process dropped the spoon and vial. The Corvette's low front overhang scraped against the blacktop and the right-side tires slipped off the road. He yanked the wheel to the left and quickly regained control.

He cursed out loud. He was going to complain to his father about the disgraceful state of the road between the airport and Magwa. He reached between his feet for the vial. It was empty. No harm done. There was plenty more at the palace, and he would be there in thirty minutes, at most. The car was intact, the air blowing at his face out of the vents was cool, and life was good.

He wondered what Jane Lambert looked like from behind, imagined her bent over, naked from the waist down, the bottom half of her scrubs down around her ankles. He felt a familiar stirring in his groin. He reached down with one hand and pulled the bottom of his *thobe* up to his thighs. That was what was best about the local garb...yes, it was comfortable and airy, but where it reigned supreme was in how it made everything so readily accessible.

***

Dr. Abdul-Razzaq Yassine was jabbing a very white juvenile Scottish buttock with a syringe when the phone on his desk rang. His nurse answered it and promptly announced that it was his wife. As instructed, she told Jane that Dr. Yassine would call her back in a few minutes. Zaig was aware that there were two other patients waiting with their mothers, so when he returned Jane's call he was intent on making it a short one. When he realized what she was calling about and understood what she was asking him to do, he could barely suppress his ire. He repeated twice that it would have to wait until after work, admonished her for wanting to get involved in the situation, then flat out told her that he had to get off the phone and attend to patients. He hung up forcefully, hating that he had to use that tone with his wife within earshot of his nurse. But it had been unavoidable. Find out the highest price ever paid for a falcon? Now? What on earth had gotten into her?

***

Salman guessed how his parents would react, and he was right. After expressing a gush of relief that he wasn't in any trouble, his mother repeatedly urged him to take the offered five hundred dinars without further ado and not risk angering the prince. She was aghast that he hadn't done so on the spot. His father had a different perspective. Five hundred dinars was a lot of money, but Salman had been right not to accept it. He was proud of his son for being a smart negotiator. This was a serious deal, and they had to get the best possible price for the falcon. His guess was they could sell it to Prince Bader for a thousand dinars, if not more. Fifteen hundred was probably off the scale. Twelve hundred sounded right as a counter offer, with a thousand being the targeted, doable deal price at which both sides would feign pain but save face.

Salman heard them both out and didn't react. Wadha insisted her husband and son had lost their minds. She warned that they were playing with fire. Faisal told her to calm down, to respect their son's desire to think about the matter, and allow him to make up his own mind.

All Salman would say was that he was undecided. He didn't mention anything about Dr. Jane's advice, but he was unquenchably curious what number she would come back to him with.

***

After seeing his last patient for the day and updating his patient files, Zaig made two calls before he left work. The first was one he wanted to make, whereby he secured an opponent for a squash match at the Hubara club for later that evening. The second he was less enthusiastic about, to a cousin who lived in Kuwait City, and of whom he requested a strange favor. He asked his cousin to make the fifteen-minute drive to the old souk near the city's waterfront, specifically to the two stalls in the bazar that were dedicated to trading in falcons, and to inquire of the proprietors as to the highest price they had ever received for a falcon. He took the return call at home, just before leaving for the squash match, and immediately relayed the information to Jane: Five thousand dinars. As he left the house he murmured that they were in the wrong business…or at least he was.

Jane was startled. She knew falconry was the sport of kings, but that was a lot of money. Did she really expect Salman to throw that number at Prince Bader? Did she want to put him in that position? She fretted as she mulled it over, but she had to decide quickly. She had told Uzi to stand by at the hospital until she called so he could in turn get word to Salman. Torn, she ultimately decided not to get entangled in the permutations of who might react how, but to tell it as it was.

Uzi dutifully ambled to the Shahab's shack and conveyed to Salman the information.

Salman was perturbed when he heard. On the one hand, he wouldn't know what to do with that kind of money, assuming Prince Bader agreed. On the other hand, the more he thought about it, the more he realized that the cause of his disquiet was the suddenly very real temptation to sell the Altai, a creature to which he had become quite attached, one that had transformed his self-image. It was as if his life had two stages, before the Altai, and now. Before, he had been nobody, a *Bidoon* that no one other than his parents and a few acquaintances knew, let alone cared about. Now, within a couple of days of trapping the falcon, Prince Bader knew who he was, and Dr. Jane knew who he was, and Uzi was running to him with important information, and...he *mattered*. The *Sinjari* had empowered him, but what would become of him if he sold it? What would it mean to be a *Bidoon* with five thousand dinars? He could buy his own brand-new Datsun pickup truck, but he would still have to stay off the roads because he couldn't buy a driver license.

When he told his mother what he'd learned from Dr. Jane, she was appalled.

"Have you lost your mind? Who are you to demand five thousand dinars from Prince Bader?"

That's exactly the point, he thought to himself. Who am I? Who am I ever going to be?

He left her beseeching him to regain his sanity. With the falcon on his wrist, he walked out beyond the edge of Magwa. The sun wouldn't set for a few hours; there were no shadows in the desert, but there was a pall hanging over him. With nothing but sand in all directions, he faced a vivid crossroads signposted in words that he—of course—could not read.

Would he ever be able to read? Would five thousand dinars be enough for him to learn to read?

He walked south and lost track of time, and after an eternity flashed by, he came to the North Ahmadi Tank Farm. His father listened to him incredulously and prayed out loud for Allah to come to the aid of his son for the momentous decision at hand. Then Salman listened while his father ran through variations of asking price and deal price and negotiating strategies and outcomes that left him dizzy and no less undecided about where he stood.

It was past midnight when Salman told his father he was heading back home.

"Take the truck," his father said. "Nobody will be on the road at this time of the night. You can come and get me in the morning."

"I will walk," Salman said. "Maybe it will clear my head."

"As you wish. Remember that you are in a good position. You stand to gain. The only question is how much."

Salman bent to pick up the falcon.

"Why don't you leave the hawk with me?" his father suggested, "so you don't have to carry it all the way back."

Salman hesitated as he thought about it. His father had a point. Besides, now that they knew what kind of money they were dealing with, better it spent the night where nobody knew it was than where at least a few interested people believed it would be. He left the falcon with his father.

He was just minutes into his return journey when he suddenly stopped, hit by an epiphany. The price was so obvious, it was amazing he hadn't seen it before! The weight of his indecision shorn, his fatigue disappeared. He walked faster, feeling he could go on forever. Now he revisited the elation he had felt two days ago when he had trapped the falcon.

As he approached Magwa, he decided not to go home. He would have to face his mother's febrile pleas, if not now then in the morning, but they would be to no avail, for his mind was set. Besides, sleep was out of the question. He pressed on, climbed the ridge towards the hospital and, like a lion spraying on another's scent, stood on the spot where Prince Bader had parked the day before. The police would go to fetch him in the morning, but he wouldn't be there; he would be here, calm, ready to look Prince Bader in the eye and name his price. With adrenaline coursing through every fiber of his being, he squatted to await the break of a new day, the dawn of a new life.

Chapter Four

Prince Bader bin Fahd Al-Dahem scratched the stubble on his chin and pondered what might well be the toughest decision he would face on any given day: Which car? Of the characteristics that set him apart, a voluntary one was a simple rule he'd conjured up upon returning from America, to never drive the same car on more than two consecutive days. Yesterday was the yellow Vette, so it was out for today. The red Vette? Or something more exotic, like the De Tomaso Mangusta? Tempting. He chuckled as he thought about why he'd ordered it. When his cousin Jasem had bought a Shelby Cobra the previous year, Bader had found him intolerably smug.

"American engine in a British car," Jasem had boasted, "The best of both worlds." So Bader did some research and discovered that "mangusta" is Italian for "mongoose", and mongooses kill cobras. Bingo.

More than any of his contemporaries, Bader nurtured an entitlement complex rooted in the conviction that he had been born in the right place at the right time. 1946 was the year Kuwait made its first international shipment of oil, opening the floodgates of fabulous wealth. With it, for the upper crust of Kuwaiti society, at the pinnacle of which was the ruling Al-Dahem family, came unprecedented power and privilege. Not all aspects of his arrival were serendipitous, for his mother did not survive the delivery. Enough distractions were lavished on the child to preclude his developing any sense of depravation. Despite the Al-Dahems' traditionally close ties to Britain, which included Kuwait being a British protectorate prior to declaring independence, in the wake of World War II, Sheikh Fahd—Bader's father—had recognized that the sun was in fact setting on the British Empire. So he shipped his callow son off for a formal education in the new epicenter of global influence, the United States. At eleven years of age Bader landed at the Hun School of Princeton. By the time he graduated from high school he had made up his mind that New Jersey was not the right fit for him—the $3,000,000 donation his father had made to Princeton University notwithstanding—and that he could best lap up those aspects of American culture that most appealed to him on the palm tree-lined boulevards of Southern California. Los Angeles meant easy access to hard-bodied women and sun-bleached boys eager to rent out their orifices, the abundance of mind-altering substances, and the perfect environment for enjoying both in fast cars under the aegis of diplomatic immunity.

Decisions, decisions. It was a mild morning, so how about a convertible? That ruled out the Mangusta. How about beyond convertible, how about the new Harley-Davidson? It had been presented to him as a graduation present by his uncle Mohammad, his father's half-brother, the prime minister and crown prince, the second most powerful man in the country. A fleet of them had been ordered for the police, but Salman's was a special edition, with his initials etched on the chrome foot rests courtesy of a compliant factory in Milwaukee. The only drawback was he wouldn't be able to transport the falcon back to the palace himself, but that was a problem easily solved. He would have his father's falcon handler follow him in the Land Cruiser to bring it home. He had already told Rashed that he was giving the *Sinjari* to his father as a birthday present, news Rashed had received enthusiastically and sworn to hold in confidence to preserve the surprise.

Helmet or no helmet?

Maybe after Magwa he would ride to Ahmadi, check out the talent around the pool at the Hubara Club. He lit a pre-breakfast joint, inhaled deeply and held his breath. When he exhaled, the familiar euphoric swell mellowed his world, and he decided. No helmet, Southern California style.

***

Salman spotted them while they were still on the road. There was the police Jeep from yesterday, the Land Cruiser he had seen leaving the hospital when he'd gone to retrieve the falcon, and leading them both, a motorcycle that emitted a deep gargling rumble like those of the police. He watched the Jeep peel away towards his home and felt a pang of guilt about how their arrival in his absence would compound his mother's angst. The motorcycle stayed on the road a little longer before turning off and heading along the dirt path to the hospital, to where he stood. Kicking up dust behind it was the Land Cruiser. Much to his surprise, it was Prince Bader, now dressed in the western mold, driving the motorcycle. He wore black leather boots and gloves and the same dark glasses, but unlike police motorcyclists, no helmet. Salman stood his ground as Prince Bader pulled up next to him and killed the engine. He gingerly leaned the motorcycle onto its stand as he checked that it wouldn't sink into the sand. Satisfied the ground was solid enough, he climbed off, removed his gloves and ran his fingers through his hair.

"Peace be upon you."

"And upon you, peace," Salman replied. He eyed the Harley's gleaming chrome.

"You are waiting for me! I take that as a good sign!"

"Whatever Allah wills," Salman said cagily.

The Land Cruiser pulled up, and its driver, the emir's falcon trainer, got out.

"Peace be upon you."

"And upon you, peace."

"Where is the *Sinjari?*" Prince Bader asked.

"It is in a safe place."

Prince Bader narrowed his eyes. "And this place is not safe?"

"Allah willing, it is safe. Allah willing, everywhere you tread will be safe."

Prince Bader nodded and studied Salman, as if enjoying the verbal tussle.

"Have you decided on a price?"

"Yes."

The prince's eyebrows shot up. "Good! How much?"

Salman glanced at the emir's falcon handler standing next to the Land Cruiser a few feet away. Prince Bader understood. He walked a few yards with Salman, their backs to the vehicles. When Prince Bader stopped, Salman knew the time had come. Cool demeanor, he told himself. Be clear and concise. "I don't want your money," he said.

Prince Bader frowned. "What does that mean?"

"I want my rights."

There was a moment of silence.

"Your rights?"

"Citizenship," Salman said. "For me and my parents."

Prince Bader was lost for words.

"And the *Sinjari* is yours," Salman added. His heart pounded, his ears rang but he showed none of it.

Prince Bader ran his palm over his mouth as he absorbed what he'd heard. Out of the slum below them the police Jeep appeared, heading in their direction.

"Where is the *Sinjari?*" Prince Bader asked again, a hint of menace in his voice.

Salman knew there was no turning back now. "It is protected, to ensure that when it becomes yours it is whole."

"We did not agree on this."

"We did not agree on anything."

"But this business…citizenship…even if it is possible, it takes time."

"With due respect, one word from you and one word from your father—"

"His Highness will not get involved in something like this!"

"Then your uncle, the prime minister; one word from him is all it would take."

Prince Bader eyed Salman incredulously. "I did not expect this from you. You can see I have brought Rashed to take the *Sinjari,* and it is my intention that you be paid handsomely for it."

"I don't want money for the hawk. I want you to have it. It will be yours, or I will release it to continue its journey."

The police Jeep pulled up next to the Land Cruiser. Two policemen got out and started to approach. Prince Bader put out a hand and they stopped.

"The *Sinjari* is not for me," Prince Bader said. "I tell you in confidence so you understand the importance of this transaction, the *Sinjari* is a gift for my father, the emir of the land."

Salman felt a pang of fear.

"When I give it to him," Prince Bader added, "I will tell him your name and your role, and he will be grateful to you."

"And I will be grateful for the citizenship. Allah willing, all will be well."

Prince Bader could have strangled Salman. "I'll tell you what," he said, "I will inquire about the citizenship, but we must agree now on a price in case it is not possible."

"I have no doubt you can make it happen," Salman insisted. "There is no need for us to discuss money."

"We will see." Prince Bader turned and strode back to Rashed and the policemen. Salman watched as they briefly exchanged words, before the prince and Rashed drove off.

The policemen got in the Jeep and drove it to Salman. "Stay close to your home," one of them said. "And if you leave, make sure your mother knows where you are." He motioned with his head to the driver, and they departed.

Salman felt elated as he watched them go. He had stayed calm and focused and made his pitch. And he was pleased that he'd kept the falcon with his father, for its absence had given him a crucial edge. *The doctor didn't show up this morning*, he thought to himself. *Just as well, for she might have been a distraction.* Now he would wait. His father would be home soon, and there was another training session with the falcon to busy himself with.

As he walked home he realized it was Thursday, which explained the doctor's no-show, for the falcon hospital was officially closed on weekends.

Salman noted that his father's pickup truck was parked at the shack. He expected to find the falcon inside, but it wasn't there. His father was eating breakfast, and his mother was clearly on edge.

"May Allah forgive you!" she cried. "All night I was waiting for you and worried that some ill had befallen you! Why didn't you tell me you weren't coming home?"

Salman kissed her on the forehead.

"Relax. I know how to look after myself." He turned to his father. "Where is the *Sinjari?*"

The old man gave him a confident nod. "Did you meet with Prince Bader?"

"Yes."

"Enlighten us."

"I gave him my proposal. He neither accepted nor rejected. He has to consult with others. We will know soon."

"Why are you hiding the hawk?" Wadha asked, suddenly alarmed by the implications.

"What is your price?" Faisal said.

"Tell me why you're hiding the hawk!"

"Because there is an ongoing negotiation," Salman said. He sat down next to his father to eat. "It is safer this way."

"How is it safer when you risk angering one of the ruling family?"

Faisal held up his hand at Wadha and turned to Salman.

"How much?"

Salman dipped a piece of bread into a bowl of yogurt and put it in his mouth. His parents watched as he chewed and swallowed. He shook his head. "My proposal does not involve money."

His parents were perplexed.

"I told him the *Sinjari* is his in exchange for citizenship for the three of us."

Faisal Shahab stared at his son in disbelief. Wadha emitted a fearful moan. "May Allah help us!" she wailed.

Salman met his father's gaze, awaiting a reaction.

Faisal smiled. "In truth? You told him that?"

Salman nodded and helped himself to another mouthful.

"May Allah bless you! Do you think he will accept?"

"We will see." Salman shrugged nonchalantly. "I told him the *Sinjari* will either become his, or I will release it."

"You have lost your mind!" Wadha said.

"It turns out he wants the *Sinjari* so he can present it as a birthday gift to his father, the Emir."

Wadha patted her cheeks with her palms in distress. "You've gone mad! Don't you—"

"In truth, this is a bold proposal!" Faisal said, drowning Wadha out. "I would not have thought of it, but if it works, our lives will change."

"If it—" Wadha started.

"We will never have a better opportunity," Salman stated flatly. "There will never again be a situation where we have something they want and cannot get anywhere else."

"You are crazy!" Wadha said, rising. "I can't bear to hear this anymore." Aghast, she draped herself with her *abaya* and left them.

"When will he respond?" Faisal asked.

"He didn't say. In the meantime, I want to continue with the training."

"As soon as you finish eating, I will take you to the hawk. May Allah bless you, my son, you are a braver man than I!"

***

Jane had never played tennis on a black asphalt court before she moved with Zaig to Kuwait and they became members of the Hubara Club. Grass was an unsustainable surface in the harsh desert environment, clay was non-existent in the country, so hard courts were the only feasible option, and asphalt was the hard court surface of choice. The ball bounced true enough, but Jane found herself taking extra care not to fall, as the surface was inherently abrasive. To that end, doubles was safer than singles, and it wasn't long before she had teamed up with her partner, Dawn, a fellow Brit, after which they quickly established themselves as a team to be reckoned with in the A bracket of the women's league. The normal schedule was a mid-week league match on Mondays or Tuesdays, under the lights after the sun had set, and a weekend social match on Thursday mornings, before it got too hot. This particular Thursday saw Jane and Dawn play against two Americans, Lisa, a redheaded Texan whose husband was a drilling safety expert, and Melanie, from Colorado, wife of a petroleum engineer. It was almost noon by the time they split the first two sets, so they all agreed to quit and cool down poolside. Sodas on ice were promptly ordered and delivered, at which point Lisa produced a flask and offered it to the others.

"Vodka," she said with a wink. "The real thing, from the embassy, although y'all didn't hear that from me!"

Dawn and Melanie availed themselves of the offer, so Jane didn't buck the trend. She had already discovered that in Kuwait, officially dry as the desert, when you could get the real thing, you took it. The more readily available alternative was "flash," the homemade variety that could hit the spot on the effect side, but invariably conceded ground on taste and aftermath. It was Jane's first social encounter with the American ladies, and after toasting each other without the visual giveaway of clinking glasses, Lisa quickly wanted the run-down on her. "How long you been here?" she asked.

"Coming on six months now," Jane said. "And you?"

"This is our fifth year. Gulf Oil originally sent us over for a three-year stint, but we enjoy it, so we're staying. What does your husband do?"

"He's a doctor."

"Yeah? What, at the hospital here?"

"Yes."

"What's y'all's last name?"

"Yassine."

Lisa put her drink down and lifted her sunglasses off her nose so Jane could see the surprise in her eyes. "What county in England is that from?" she said.

Jane kept her glasses on and smiled. "My husband is Kuwaiti."

"No shit! Well, I don't mean it to sound like…I mean…it's cool, you know?"

"Where did you meet?" Melanie asked.

"In England," Jane replied. She was beyond being surprised at the reactions of others.

"And Jane is also a doctor," Dawn interjected. "She's an avian veterinarian. And she's running a falcon hospital. You know that hut on the hill at Magwa, on the way to the airport, where the old hospital used to be?"

"Yeah."

"I hear it's the world's first hospital dedicated to the care of falcons. Is that right?" Dawn looked at Jane, who nodded.

"No shit!" Lisa said again. "How'd that come about?"

Dawn sensed that Jane hadn't warmed up to Lisa, so she replied for her.

"The Emir himself commissioned Jane to do this. He's apparently addicted to falconry."

"That's not the only thing he's addicted to, from what I hear!" Lisa said. She lowered her voice. "Rumor has it the sumbitch sleeps with a different woman every Thursday!"

Dawn and Melanie had heard the rumor before, so it was only Jane who was taken aback.

"And not only a different woman," Lisa added with bemused indignation, "a different *virgin!*"

Jane couldn't believe what she was hearing. She decided not to dignify the gossip with a response.

"Have you met him?" Lisa asked.

"Yes," Jane replied. "A very sincere, kind and considerate man, from what I've seen."

"So he's your boss?"

"Oh, I wouldn't say that. I just tend to his sick falcons. His and anyone else's."

"Well don't you be telling him I said anything now!" Lisa said. She took another sip of her drink. "Like I said, we like it here."

Jane rolled her eyes.

"Hey!" Lisa went on. "It's Thursday!"

"So?" Dawn asked.

"So I wonder what the Emir's doin' tonight! More to the point, I wonder *who* he's doin' tonight!" She squealed with laughter.

Jane got up. "I enjoyed the tennis, ladies."

"Don't be taking offence, Jane," Lisa said. "It's all just good-natured fun in the sun, that's all."

"Too much sun for me, I'm afraid," Jane said as she gathered her things. "I'm off."

As Jane walked away, Lisa reached for Jane's glass and poured its contents into her own. "That lady's gonna have to learn to chill!" she said.

***

Prince Bader rode through Ahmadi in a funk. Had things gone the way he had planned, by now the *Sinjari* would have been in safe keeping at the palace, ready to be gifted to his father. By now he would have forgotten that he'd ever met Salman Shahab and his mind would have been unencumbered by unfinished business. He thrived on being a man who did things because he wanted to, not because he *had* to.

He pulled over into the parking lot of the Cricket Ground and parked in a secluded corner shaded by tall eucalyptus trees. He turned the engine off, rested the Harley on its kickstand, and considered the best way to approach his uncle.

He could call him, but the timing had to be right; he couldn't be interrupting anything. On the other hand, this was not a subject for a telephone conversation. He could go to his uncle's Thursday evening *diwaniya*, the traditional weekly town-hall style gathering at which they could talk face-to-face, and he would have his uncle's undivided attention for at least a few minutes, long enough to explain the situation and pose the question. The drawback was that government ministers, politicians and prominent businessmen attended Thursday *diwaniyas*. Too many would be within earshot. The Friday gatherings were family affairs, so they entailed fewer people and were more conducive to a private sidebar conference. It would be better to wait until tomorrow, but the clock was ticking, and with his father's birthday only days away, he wanted this whole business settled sooner rather than later. He decided to go to the *diwaniya* tonight and force the issue.

This whole business was tiresome. Fuck you, Salman Shahab.

***

Salman started as he had the day before, by calling out the falcon's name and stroking her plumage. She readily accepted the first piece of meat. He watched her swallow as he fished the hood out of his pocket. He positioned himself to her right and slipped the hood over her eyes. Resuming the previous day's routine, he removed the hood and replayed the cycle to the mantra of her name. The key was gentle persistence. It wasn't about breaking her will or matching wits with her, but about making her comfortable with him. Good practice for dealing with any female, he mused.

For twenty minutes he placed and removed the hood. Eventually, with it on her, he pulled the leather drawstrings at the back and tightened it to a snug fit. He stepped back, alert for signs of distress. She was calm. He had timed it to perfection.

He donned the cuff and eased her off the *wakir* onto his arm. She reacted with a brief flare of her wings, a gesture of mild protest before she settled down again. Salman paced around slowly, brushing her with the feather and calling out her name. He waited longer this time before loosening the drawstrings and removing the hood. She could see him better now, the sag of her eyelids allowing clearer image definition by the day. He busied her with another piece of meat and slipped the hood back on.

So it went for an hour, from cuff to *wakir* and back again. As she grew more receptive, she began to react to her name. He figured it would be another two days before her eyelids sagged enough to fully restore her vision, by which time she would have become acclimated to the hood. He hoped that by then she would no longer be his.

***

Prince Bader spent the rest of the morning riding. East from Ahmadi, then south on the coast road, towards the Neutral Zone, the area shared by Kuwait and Saudi Arabia, along the stretch where the frontier between the two countries was undefined. Two American companies, Aminoil and Getty, had petroleum exploration concessions in the area, and he wanted to see for himself how their compounds compared with Ahmadi. He discovered they were at best very minor siblings. As he rode back north toward Kuwait City, he made a mental note to talk to his father about two things. First, the urgent need to implement mandatory driver education. The citizens *had* to be taught to drive between the traffic lane markings on the roads instead of centering their cars on them. Second, the country was in dire need of a system for disposing of the detritus of automobile wrecks that defaced the roadways left and right.

Back at the palace, he smoked another joint, ate lunch and took a nap. When he awoke he showered and shaved, all the while grappling with a nagging question: What if his uncle said no?

Seating at the *diwaniya* was arranged on three sides of a rectangle, two long sides flanking a short one, at the midpoint of which sat the crown prince. When Prince Bader arrived, his uncle rose to greet him, and all the other men in the room followed suit. Sheikh Mohammad indicated that Prince Bader was to sit next to him and the seat was promptly vacated. When Sheikh Mohammad sat, it was the cue for the rest of the gathered menfolk. A few minutes of courteous small talk ensued, Sheikh Mohammad inquiring about Prince Bader's time in the States, the latter responding with a brief account sanitized by the omission of transgressions. In due course Sheikh Mohammad sent out a subtle signal indicating he was open to the approach of one particular dignitary for greetings. The stand-and-sit routine played out again, and the cycle repeated. Prince Bader was on the verge of abandoning his mission out of a sense it was the wrong time and place when his uncle sensed he was not there merely for a show of courtesy and respect. "What is on your mind?" Sheikh Mohammad asked.

The opening was the icebreaker Prince Bader needed. "No, by Allah, nothing," he said. "Just a small matter that is hardly worthy of your bother."

"No matter that concerns you is a bother for me."

Sheikh Mohammad had spoken softly, but he hadn't moved. Prince Bader leaned towards his uncle, indicating that the small matter was a private one. Sheikh Mohammad reciprocated, albeit to a lesser extent.

"You know it is my father's birthday in a few days."

The older man nodded.

"I want to gift him a rare hawk, a *Sinjari.*"

"That is appropriate. I don't believe he has one."

"I have found a remarkable *Sinjari.*"

"Excellent!"

"But to acquire it...I need your assistance, Uncle."

Sheikh Mohammad knew it wasn't about money. He awaited the inevitable clarification.

"This *Sinjari* was trapped a few days ago, in the desert near Magwa, by a boy."

The crown prince's attention was total.

"I offered to buy it, but the boy's price is beyond my means."

Sheikh Mohammad raised an eyebrow.

"He is *Bidoon*. He will trade the *Sinjari* to me…in return for citizenship for his parents and himself."

Sheikh Mohammad reverted to his prior posture and looked away. There was no doubt the body language was one of disapproval.

"Of course, I have not agreed!" Prince Bader hastened to add. "I wanted first to consult you. You know how much I respect you…and your wisdom."

When he turned back to face his nephew, Sheikh Mohammad was stone-faced.

"What is the boy's name?"

"Salman Shahab."

Sheikh Mohammad grunted. "Shahab. Iranian." After a pause he added, "Shia."

"As I said, I—"

"Enough." Sheikh Mohammad shook his head almost imperceptibly. "Not here."

Prince Bader didn't see the signal, but his uncle had given one because two men rose from their seats at a far corner and approached. Before he stood to greet them, Sheikh Mohammad ended his conversation with his nephew with a curt, "We will talk tomorrow."

Chapter Five

Sheikh Fahd bin Khaled Al-Dahem glanced up at the gold-plated clock mounted on the wall across the room from his desk, saw that it was already past six, and decided to call it a day. He had been at it for twelve hours, breaking only to eat and to pray, the usual routine behind his workaholic reputation. Devoid as they were of the weekday lineups of meetings and receptions with the endless stream of dignitaries and delegations, Thursdays always presented an opportunity to catch up on paperwork, mainly perusal of briefs written by aides and advisers outlining the issues to be considered to make his decisions informed. The remaining open file before him posed an interesting quandary, the likes of which he hadn't previously encountered. His cousin, the minister for sport and recreation, was proposing that Kuwait donate to Muhammad Ali the $280,000 the deposed world heavyweight boxing champion owed to his lawyers after being sentenced to five years in jail for refusing to serve with the US military in Vietnam. Like everyone else in Kuwait, indeed in the larger Arab and Muslim world, the minister considered Muhammad Ali a hero, not only for his exploits in the ring, but for the righteousness he displayed when he embraced Islam, and for his rectitude in subsequently defending the faith. This would be a gesture that would resonate around the world. All it lacked was approval by the Emir.

 Sheikh Fahd leaned back in his chair and rubbed his eyes. He too considered Muhammad Ali a hero, an icon of sports and humanity. And while he had reservations about the Nation of Islam organization Ali was affiliated with, he did feel it was incumbent on Muslims to show him solidarity. But the financial support the minister was asking for was problematic. It was too overt, and thus risked rubbing the American government the wrong way. The Emir considered his role to be one of benevolent custodianship of Kuwait's land and resources, and all decisions had to be weighed in the context of the national interest. In the years before independence, Kuwait had been a British protectorate, but these were different times, and now it was relations with America that demanded the highest degree of discernment and tact. Kuwait couldn't be seen to be meddling in an internal matter, a legal dispute between the American government and an American citizen, regardless who the latter might be. He penned a pithy articulation of his dissent on the minister's memorandum and closed the leather-bound folder. Using the intercom on his desk he summoned an aide who appeared within seconds.

"Get Mansour on a private line," the Emir said as the aide gathered the stack of folders.

"Immediately, your Highness."

There were four telephones on the Emir's desk, two black handsets, two red. The black phones were for calls that could have multiple participants, like conference calls, or for conversations he would allow, usually by invitation only, aides or cabinet members to listen in on. The red ones were private lines, for calls between the Emir and one person on the other end, be it a head of state or someone in the next room. He never used more than one at a time; the duplicates were simply for redundancy, lest a line or handset suffer a technical glitch.

"At your convenience, your Highness," the aide's voice announced on the intercom.

He reached for the primary red phone. "Everything ready?"

"Yes, your Highness."

"What is her name?"

"Badriyya."

"Her age?"

"Fifteen."

He emitted a sigh of contentment.

"Anything I need to know?"

"She has been briefed. The dowry has been paid. She is ready."

With a satisfied nod, the Emir dropped the handset on the cradle. He rose and walked to the wooden oriel window and gazed out at the still waters of the gulf. It was always a special thrill when someone new became a recipient of his largesse.

The office suite was separated from his personal chamber by a long hallway, by any measure an epitome of opulence, lined with expensive antiques and works of art, the floor a sumptuous array of rare Persian carpets, none of which Badriyya would have seen. Her passage to the apartment she was ensconced in had taken a more subdued, direct route, obscured behind tinted windows as she had been chauffeured through the perimeter gate then ushered through a nondescript side door the Emir had inserted during the last renovation, specifically for the purpose, along with the soundproofing. He found her waiting as she had been told to wait, seated awkwardly on the bed, as if to preclude any vestige of doubt as to why she was there.

It was a given that no one in their right mind would dare enter the apartment without his express permission, but still he locked the door to the hallway and the only other door, the one to the carport. When he stood at the foot of the bed she dropped her veil.

"I marry you, myself," she said, just as she had been instructed, her face aquiver.

In stature, physicality, and authority, he towered over her. Starting every Saturday morning, and for six days of each week, he was bound by the demands of his position, one bestowed upon him the moment his predecessor had chosen him as crown prince. For six out of every seven days, he was privileged to be the face of the nation, at the cost of being in the limelight. But he had long established that come Thursday evening, the official demands of state protocol would be set aside so he could act less leader of the country, more alpha of the pride.

She looked up at him meekly, and his eyes directed hers down to his groin, to the burgeoning bulge billowing his *thobe*. With a gasp she reeled back.

Their reaction was always the same. Relishing the thought of what was to come, he said with a wry smile, "I accept."

Chapter Six

On Friday morning, four days after Salman trapped the falcon, the sag of her eyelids was almost complete. He had expected it would be Saturday morning before her pupils were wholly visible, but now there they were.

"It is time to remove the string," his father said.

Salman had never done it before on a live falcon. She was mildly agitated, so he paused to give her time to settle down. Tethered to the perch, she was not going anywhere.

"Keep talking when you are around the hawk," Faisal said. "Accustoming it to the sounds it will hear when you take it to hunt is part of the training, and your voice is the most important one."

"I know," Salman said. "I'm concentrating."

"Do you have your dagger?"

Salman reached into his gear bag and pulled out a dagger with a five-inch handle and a six-inch curved blade.

"Is it sharp?"

Salman gave his father a glance of respectful reproach. "It is always sharp."

She was calm now when he approached. He raised the string where it was knotted above her head and sliced through it with one deft stroke of the dagger. He gently pulled the string out of her eyelids and stepped back.

"Good," said his father.

"First time I see her eyes since she was in the net."

Salman called out her name and started pacing around her. She turned her head to follow him with her gaze.

"It is amazing how they rotate their heads almost full-circle."

She fluttered her wings and shifted restlessly on the perch. Salman fished the hood out of his pocket.

"Yesterday she took it for as long as fifteen minutes."

"Good," his father said. "Today try to leave it on for up to an hour, but no more."

Salman positioned himself to her right and slipped the hood over her head, quickly tightening it to a snug fit. The loss of her eyesight had an immediate calming effect.

"I leave you now," Faisal said.

As his father turned to go, Salman said, "Do you think I will hear from Prince Bader today?"

"Maybe, if he has spoken with his uncle."

For Salman, the weight of the wait was acute, but it was pointless to bare it to his father.

"If not, I will start training it with the *tilwah*, this afternoon," he said.

"You will have to take it outside for that," said his father. Training with a lure required sand underfoot.

Salman nodded. "Allah is benevolent."

For close to an hour they remained together, Salman and the hooded falcon, and she remained calm. He had purposely not fed her before removing the thread, knowing that she would be easier to handle when hungry. The tactic proved its worth, as she showed no more edginess when he removed the hood. Now he gave her a strip of pigeon meat and she gulped it down. He stroked her plumage and called out her name. He hooded and un-hooded her a few more times, leaving the hood on a few minutes each time, delighting in how comfortable she was with it. It was an important milestone in her training, for it meant she was ready for him to take it to the next level.

***

Before he met Jane Lambert at the student union at Birmingham University, Zaig Yassine had imagined he would return to his homeland after finishing medical school and practice at one of the new hospitals the government had commissioned in Kuwait City. He had anticipated living in one of the new government-subsidized housing complexes close to his parents' villa, getting married, and starting a family. But love's intervention changed his plans. While employment at Kuwait Oil Company offered him the opportunity to work in Kuwait's newest hospital, it had the added bonus of residence in Ahmadi, where the predominance of westerners would mitigate his wife's inevitable culture shock. The downside was the one-hour drive to Kuwait City meant he would only see his parents on weekends, on Fridays as it turned out, when he and Jane would visit for lunch with the extended family, as they were on their way to do now. They were on the coast road, Zaig behind the wheel of his white Chevrolet company car, Jane next to him in the passenger seat. He glanced at her.

"Something is bothering you."

Jane knew she had made it obvious. Now it was time to get it off her chest.

"Is it true the Emir sleeps with a different virgin every Thursday?"

"What?" Zaig said, floored by the question. "Where did you hear that?"

"At the club. Yesterday. After tennis. One of the ladies."

Zaig shot her a bemused look. "Really!"

"Is it true?"

"Darling, how would I know?"

"Do you think it could be true?"

He sighed. "I don't know. I mean…it could be. You know, executive privilege, that sort of thing."

"Are you serious?"

He shrugged.

"No, really. Do you think he does?"

"Who knows?"

"I'd be appalled if it were true."

"It's not our business to—"

"It would be decadent and immoral."

Zaig fell silent. Some cultural differences were bound to be unbridgeable.

"Say something!" Jane said.

"What do you want me to say?"

"Don't you agree?"

"Jane, don't be judgmental. We don't know the—"

"This is bizarre, Zaig. Don't you have an opinion?"

"My opinion is, like I've told you before, there are cultural norms that might not be…that you might not be comfortable with—"

"Oh for God's sake! Is it a cultural norm for a man to sleep with a different virgin every week? Would that appeal to you?"

"I think I could handle it," Zaig said with a chuckle.

"Come on, be serious. Do you think it's defensible that he does it because he's the Emir?"

It was not a conversation he was enjoying, but Zaig knew he had to see it through. "There's something called the pleasure marriage."

"*Pleasure* marriage?"

"*Zawaj al muta'ah*. A man and a woman enter into a consensual agreement, a temporary marriage for their mutual pleasure."

Jane was flabbergasted.

"And then they divorce."

She looked at him in disbelief. "Isn't he married?"

"No. He only had one wife, and she died giving birth to Bader."

"So now he gets married every weekend."

Again Zaig shrugged.

"Is it legal?"

"Debatable. It's more prevalent amongst Shias, much less so amongst Sunnis, but we're talking about the Emir. Who dares challenge him with legalities?"

"I think it's very sad, very troubling."

There was nothing more Zaig cared to add.

"What happens to the women after he divorces them?"

"Life goes on."

"For him, no doubt. For them?"

"For both of them."

"You said it was consensual. Do the women have a choice?"

"Both parties have to agree to the marriage. That is part of the mechanics of the arrangement."

"Well, it certainly does sound mechanical."

Zaig's indulgence was wearing thin. "I don't like it when you get cynical and sarcastic," he said dryly.

"And I don't like it when you are blasé about indecency!"

"OK. So, let's drop the subject so we can keep liking each other."

Quiet descended upon them. Zaig turned on the radio, and not another word was spoken for the rest of the drive.

***

Prince Bader awoke in a daze. His mind cleared as soon as he remembered what had induced the night of fitful sleep. He replayed last evening's episode and his mood turned dour.

For starters, it was time to acknowledge that he'd let himself down. The adage about never mixing business with pleasure was true. It had been a mistake to smoke a joint before riding out to Magwa yesterday, because hashish mellowed him out and dulled his edge. It made everything hunky-dory—as Americans like to say—when it wasn't. He had been caught off guard by Salman Shahab's demand, otherwise he would have rejected it on the spot. Raising the issue with his uncle had been more than another mistake, it had been an embarrassment. He should have known better. There was a small chance his uncle would humor him and grant him this favor, only because the *Sinjari* was destined for his father, but he wouldn't bet on it. Still, it was now incumbent on him to hang around the palace and await his uncle's call, the call that would likely confirm what an idiot he had been. But he could fix this. He had to quit fucking around, be decisive and redeem himself. He had shown the *Bidoon* boy too much respect. He knew exactly what he needed to do to set things straight.

The decision to take things into his own hands lifted his gloom and restored his equilibrium. He got out of bed and rolled a joint.

***

It was late afternoon when Salman climbed in behind the wheel of the Datsun and tossed his gear bag into the passenger seat. He whistled out loud, then cranked the engine. Hamza ran out of his parent's shack.

"Where is the *Sinjari*? Did you sell it to the prince?"

"Not yet," replied Salman, looking beyond Hamza in the hope that Hissa would appear.

"Have you been training it without me? You have, haven't you?"

"I'm going now to introduce it to the lure. Do you want to come?"

Sure enough, Hissa came to the entrance to the shack and looked out, as if checking on her brother. Salman smiled at her.

Hamza clambered into the passenger seat before Salman could change his mind. "Where is the *Sinjari*?"

"You'll see. But first you have to swear not to tell anyone."
"I swear!"
"Not even your parents."
"No one!"

Salman engaged first gear and eased his foot off the clutch. Hissa adjusted the *abaya* on her head, and in so doing exposed just enough of her face for Salman to see that she was returning his smile.

***

Zaig's parents had initially reacted with dismay to the news that their older son wanted to marry an Englishwoman. Zaig had been respectful enough to ask for their permission, although it quickly became clear that his heart was set. Or stolen, as his mother had put it. Zaig managed to convince them to meet Jane before passing judgment, which they did a few months later in London, whereupon they relented. It had helped that she'd made a concerted effort to learn Arabic, an undertaking that had paid dividends in charm points and had showcased her intelligence. Her good looks and engaging personality were factors, but the clincher had been her readiness to convert to Islam. That had been critical for them, so she had willingly recited the dozen-or-so words about bearing witness that there is but one God and that Muhammad is his prophet. She had not, at that time or in the two years since, let on to them that for her it was merely a matter of going through the motions.

There had been no culture shock to speak of when she had moved to Kuwait with Zaig, in large part due to the Anglo-American oasis of Ahmadi. The Fridays spent at Zaig's parents' house were fine; their hospitality was such that she was always made to feel not only at home, but like a favored child. Far from being uncomfortable in Kuwait, she felt more coddled by the local warmth and pampered by the oil company perks than she'd dared to imagine. Except for the past few days, when she'd learned about the *Bidoon* and the Emir's sexual proclivities, revelations that bothered her now in two ways. First, they had created some friction between her and Zaig that hadn't existed before. Second, the fact that she was essentially employed by the Emir was arguably an endorsement of behavior she considered reprehensible. Now, sipping afternoon tea with her mother-in-law, she found herself torn between accepting things as they were, and taking a stand that risked alienating Zaig and his family. She loved Zaig and cared deeply for these wonderful people, and she could not countenance causing them discomfort, let alone pain. It occurred to her that her conflicting emotions may just well be what culture shock is all about.

***

Salman let Hamza thrust a *wakir* into the sand, then deposited the falcon on it. From the gear bag he retrieved a tangle of black-spotted white and brown Houbara feathers sewn to the end of a cord, and a nylon bag containing pigeon meat. He tied a strip of the meat in amongst the feathers. He removed the falcon's hood, took a couple of steps back and called out: "Altai!"

The falcon gave him the usual haughty glare and jumped off the *wakir*. Salman tossed the lure onto the sand. The falcon's head bobbed up and down as it eyed the feathers, then it stepped away. Hamza held his breath, his eyes flitting from the falcon to Salman and back again. Still she eyed the lure without touching it, as if waiting for the object at her feet to make the first move. Thirty seconds ticked by, forty-five, a minute. Salman remained still and fixated on the falcon, as if willing her to pounce. Sure enough, the instant she realized there was meat in the feathers, pounce she did. With a quick hop she was on the lure and picking at the meat. She flicked a chunk into the concave cavity of her beak before dislodging it with her tongue and swallowing it.

Salman's eyes twinkled with excitement. He let her have another bite. "Watch now!" he said.

With his foot he brushed sand over the lure and covered it while the falcon was savoring the meat. When she looked down again the feathers were gone. Salman crouched and held out his arm.

"Altai!"

Confused by the disappearance of the food, the hawk hesitated, then she stepped onto the cuff. Salman was ready with another morsel of meat that he laid on her talons. He let her devour it before fitting the hood back on her head.

"That's all for today," Salman said. "Tomorrow I'll put her on a longer cord and set the lure farther away. When she comes for it, it'll be her last meal from the feathers."

"Just the two times is enough?" Hamza said.

"Yes. The goal is to make the lure a homing beacon, not a feeding plate. It is just to attract the hawk's attention and bring her back, no more."

Later, when they were in the pickup, Hamza said, "I know why you are hiding the *Sinjari*."

Salman glanced at him.

"You fear the prince will take it and not pay you."

Salman groaned inwardly. He began to think it had been a mistake to bring Hamza along.

"Silence is assent," the boy said.

"Enough," said Salman. "Just remember you gave me your word."

"I won't tell."

Salman caught the boy's smug smile, the smile of someone whose hunch had just been confirmed.

***

It was early evening when a valet notified Prince Bader via intercom that His Excellency the Crown Prince was on the line. Sheikh Mohammad was crisp and to the point: Salman Shahab's proposition was a non-starter; there could be no negotiation with any of the *Bidoon* about anything. He gently admonished his nephew for apparently letting his time in America blunt his instincts for what is admissible in Kuwait, and more importantly, what is not. Then he hung up.

Prince Bader was left smarting. He had correctly guessed what his uncle's response to Shahab's request would be, but hearing his uncle question his judgment…that hurt. The remedy came back into focus. No more respect for the *Bidoon* boy. He was just going to take the *Sinjari*. What could the boy do? Go to the police?

There was only one problem. He didn't know where the *Sinjari* was.

It had to be in Magwa. Where else could it be? It was in one of those filthy shacks, and he would find it. Or to be more precise, the police would.

Chapter Seven

Sheikh Fahd bin Khaled Al-Dahem was habitually an early riser, particularly on Saturdays, when he would make getting a jump on the start of the workweek his first order of business. Up before first dawn, he took a quick shower and dried himself off just as the light spread upward in the sky from the east, perfect timing to complete the first of his five daily prayers before sunrise. As he strapped on his watch, the cadence of the girl's breathing told him she was still in deep slumber. He gazed at her and instantly felt the pings of re-arousal.

He had long accepted his drive as a vagary of the human condition, a bodily need that had to be serviced, much like hunger and thirst, only unquenchable without the essential spice of variety. They were a mismatch, as were most women next to a man of his size, but more so Badriyya, because she was so petite. On Thursday he had quickly given up on any thoughts of penetration for fear of harming her. With her own fears thus assuaged, she had in turn submitted to his every whim with alternate means of gratification that rendered him nominally satisfied, albeit temporarily.

He slid the sheet off her and gently pulled her towards him by her ankles while admiring her suppleness. She awoke, tensed for a moment, then recognized her surroundings and allowed her body to go limp, her mind to numb.

"I divorce you," he said.

She heard the words and looked up at him for the last time.

He left the room not knowing whether the flicker in her eyes spoke of grief or gratitude.

Chapter Eight

They swept up from Ahmadi at an early hour, five police Jeeps in single file. One peeled off and parked on the side of the road just south of Magwa, another drove straight through and parked on the ridge next to the hospital on the north side of town. A third assumed a vigil post at the western perimeter and a fourth mirrored it to the east. All parked facing Magwa, eight policemen in all, eyes peeled for anyone trying to leave the slum in any direction. All communicated via wireless radio back to Prince Bader, overseeing the operation from behind the desk of the chief at the Ahmadi Police Station. The two remaining policemen in the fifth Jeep took the shortest route to the Shahab's shack and proceeded to enter with neither notice nor hesitation. They found only the woman of the household home.

Wadha worse fears flared as she sensed that the gloves had come off.

"Where's your son?" a brusque brute in uniform demanded of her.

"I don't know," she replied, hastily covering her head with her *abaya*. "I beg of you, he has done nothing—"

"Shut up! He has stolen the prince's falcon and he must return it!"

"But he trapped—"

"He trapped it after the prince trapped it first and it escaped! It belongs to Prince Bader! If your son turns in the falcon before we arrest him, there will be no trouble and he will be allowed to go free."

They left Wadha distraught and anguished. She heard the doors of the Jeep slam.

"Residents of Magwa!" The voice, amplified by a megaphone, sent shudders of fear rippling through Wadha's body. "Listen, oh residents of Magwa! The boy Salman Shahab is in possession of a stolen falcon, a falcon belonging to Prince Bader bin-Fahd Al Dahem! Anyone who leads us to him will be rewarded. Anyone who shelters him will be punished!"

Wadha was wide-eyed with terror. As the Jeep rolled away, the voice on the megaphone blurted out: "We will search your homes. Any home found to be hiding Salman Shahab or the prince's falcon will be burned to the ground! If you are sheltering him surrender him now and save yourself and your home!"

A few souls succumbed to curiosity and ventured out of their shacks. One of them waited until the Jeep had turned a corner and disappeared from view before running to the Shahab's shack. Hamza stuck a head inside, found Wadha moaning, saw that she was alone, and left. He walked with purpose to the eastern edge of town and slowed down when he saw the Jeep parked beyond the perimeter. He kept walking. A policeman got out of the Jeep and shouted at him: "Boy! Where are you going?"

"Beyond the dunes," Hamza replied. "I have to do my morning business!" He grabbed his crotch.

The policeman scowled and got back in the Jeep.

Hamza walked until he was beyond the first dune and out of sight of the policemen, then he raised his *thobe* above his knees and started running for all he was worth.

***

The shallow gully in the desert a few miles north of Ahmadi was out of sight from the surrounding area, so well situated for today's session. Salman stuck a *wakir* into the sand and put the falcon on it. The bird was hooded, but still Salman tethered the jesses around its legs to the leash attached to the perch through a swivel and grommet. Today's mission was simply to increase the distance the falcon had to cover to reach the lure, while simultaneously consolidating her association of the lure with food. As his father watched, Salman retrieved the lure from the gear back and tied into the feathers a freshly cut strip of pigeon meat. Salman paced out five full-stride steps beyond the perch, then turned to his father and nodded.

Standing next to the falcon, Faisal shook his head.

"What is it?" Salman said.

"The cord."

Salman suddenly realized he was about to tempt the falcon to fly five yards to the lure while attached to the perch with a five-foot cord. He smiled sheepishly. He dropped the lure and pulled a longer creance line out of the gear bag.

"Not thinking," he muttered as he switched the cords. When he was done, he loosened the braces on the hood and left it loose on the falcon's head. He walked back to the lure, picked it up and performed a final check: meat in the Houbara wings, thirty-yard leash, cuff donned, hood loose. Now when he looked at his father, the old man nodded.

Faisal stood to the falcon's right. He reached out and removed the hood. Salman dangled the lure from its cord and swung it like a pendulum at his knees. The raptor's head jerked once before she focused on the mass of feathers. Salman called out her name and dropped the lure to the sand.

The falcon lurched off the perch and landed with backswept wings, her talons thrust out in front of her like a slew of rapiers. The impact was emphatic, and she wasted no time pecking through the feathers to scavenge the meat. When she pulled up to swallow Salman brushed his foot across the sand, covering the lure beneath her. He crouched down, offered his arm and called to her again. She stepped onto the cuff and was rewarded with a gobbet of meat.

Salman removed the remnants of the meat from the lure and they repeated the process twice, each time doubling the distance between the perch and the lure. Conditioned by the accumulation of stress-induced fatigue in her fifth day of captivity, the falcon responded on cue. By the time they wrapped up the session, father and son were both satisfied that the hawk was now accustomed to the lure, and therefore ready for the next training milestone: free, cordless flight.

They drove back to the tank farm, arriving just moments before the first Bechtel construction bus turned off the main road towards them.

"Hurry," Faisal said.

Salman wasted no time. With the falcon on his wrist and his gear bag slung over his shoulder he ascended the steps curving up the side of one of the unfinished tanks and disappeared over the rim. He reappeared a few seconds later, now without the falcon and gear bag, and scampered back down the steps to the ground. By the time the bus arrived at the security gate, the white Datsun pickup had already left the tank farm and turned north onto the dirt road in the direction of Magwa.

***

When she sat down for breakfast with Zaig on Saturday, Jane had already rationalized her feelings.

"In life there is the big picture, and many little ones," she said as she poured two cups of tea.

"True." Zaig stirred two teaspoons of sugar into his cup while Jane added one to hers and whitened it with milk.

"My big picture is you, your happiness, your family, our health, and the life we've chosen to live here together," Jane said.

He reached out and squeezed her hand.

"In recent days I've let a few things upset me," she continued. "The *Bidoon* thing, and the Emir's private life. Those are little pictures."

Zaig waited as she took a sip of her tea.

"I won't let the little pictures cloud the big one."

Their eyes met in harmony.

"I love you deeply," Zaig said. "And your happiness is *my* big picture."

Some twenty minutes later, on her approach to Magwa, Jane noticed the first hint that something was amiss. A police Jeep parked by the side of the road, another parked in the opposite direction on the hillock in front of the hospital. She looked around from that elevation and noticed the other two, to the east and west.

"Do you know why there are police Jeeps around Magwa?" she asked Uzi when she walked in.

"No madam doctor."

"Come and see."

They stepped out and walked around the side of the Quonset hut. Uzi saw what she was talking about.

"It's very unusual," Jane said.

"Yes. Shall I ask them?"

Mindful of that morning's conversation with Zaig, Jane said, "Come back inside."

In the time it took them to walk back inside to the lobby, curiosity got the better of her. She decided there was a difference between interfering in someone else's business and simply trying to find out what was happening on your doorstep. As long as she stayed on the right side of that line…

"Go down to Salman's place and find out if this has anything to do with him and the Altai."

"What if they stop me?"

"You tell them you are going to check the Altai's feathers. A medical visit. Go."

A pang of apprehension rippled through Uzi. He worked at the Emir's falcon hospital, so he felt he was safe. His only hope was that if this did in fact have anything to do with the Altai, he would be spared from an encounter with Prince Bader. He took a step towards the door, then stopped.

"It is better if I take something."

He went into the exam room and emerged a few seconds later with a stethoscope around his neck. "Better, no?"

Jane smiled. "Good man."

***

The word that came back over the wireless radio was not what Prince Bader wanted to hear. There was no sign of Salman Shahab or his *Sinjari* falcon in Magwa. A thorough search would require a methodical sweep through each and every shack, a proposition that would in turn require a far larger police presence on the ground than was currently available. The announcement and warning had been made repeatedly through the megaphone as instructed, to no avail. The perimeter watch was still in effect. All units were awaiting further instructions.

It was as Prince Bader had feared. He had sensed that the Shahab boy was, true to his desert roots, a wily character. He hadn't been bluffing when he'd said the *Sinjari* was in a safe place; what he'd meant was that it was safely secreted away. It was either hidden somewhere in Magwa, in which case the megaphone announcement would hopefully put the fear of punitive retribution in the hearts of anyone abetting the boy, or it was hidden elsewhere, in which case finding it was going to be impossible without inside help, which meant putting fear in the hearts of those who might know where it was hidden. Like the boy's parents, or his falconer friends. And of course, there was the boy himself. Salman Shahab was still waiting to hear a response to his proposal, so *he* wouldn't be in hiding.

But if word got to him about the announcement through the megaphone, he would know what the response was, and that might force him into hiding.

Shit.

Prince Bader cringed as the anger welled inside him. That had been a miscalculation. He wanted to be a step ahead of Shahab, not the other way around. Assuming the boy was now in hiding, the best bet was to get to his parents. The boy had the brashness of youth about him, but his father would surely be more level-headed, more fearful of defying authority.

"Go back to the Shahab house," Prince Bader shouted into the wireless. "Find out the boy's father's name and find out where he is. If he is in the house, hold him. I am on my way."

It was an age-old truth: To force a parent's hand, threaten the child with harm. Prince Bader strode out of the Ahmadi Police Station with every intention of proving that the reverse was also true.

***

The policemen watching Magwa's perimeter had been told to intercept anyone fitting Salman Shahab's description, or anyone with a falcon, if they tried to leave town. Nothing had been said about anyone entering Magwa. And so it was that the white Datsun pickup truck approaching from the southeast on a dirt track drove past the police Jeep stationed on that side of town noticed but unhindered. It negotiated a few turns, then came to a stop in front of a shack where several curious onlookers had gathered. Bodies shuffled to one side as Faisal Shahab stepped out of the vehicle and made his way to the shack. Scant attention was paid to Hamza, who also got out of the pickup and waited apart from the loiterers. Just as the rising voices of an acrimonious exchange began to filter out of the shack, they were drowned out by the sound of the returning police Jeep. The loiterers dispersed. Moments later the eyes peering out from the long morning shadows witnessed Faisal Shahab being escorted into the back of the Jeep. Wadha emerged from the shack, alternately remonstrating and pleading with the policemen. Suddenly a new face appeared on the scene, an Asian man, incongruous with the surroundings in his medical scrubs and stethoscope. Uzi slowed down when he saw the police. He took in the sight of Wadha in distress, then noticed the little boy next to the pickup. He approached Hamza.

"What is happening?"

Hamza looked at him warily.

"I am from the hospital," Uzi said. "Where is Salman?"

"Not here."

"Why are the police here?"

Hamza was hesitant.

"Do you know what is happening?" Uzi persisted.

"They are looking for the *Sinjari*."

Uzi instinctively swallowed. "Why?"

"They say it belongs to Prince Bader."

Uzi was shocked. "But wasn't it Salman who trapped it?"

Hamza didn't know whose side Uzi was on. He shrugged his shoulders.

"Do you know where the *Sinjari* is?" said Uzi.

Again Hamza hesitated; again he shrugged.

Uzi began to wonder how truthful the boy was, but his thoughts were sidetracked when another police Jeep suddenly careened around the corner, barely avoiding a collision with the pickup. It skidded to a stop behind the first Jeep.

Prince Bader saw Uzi before Uzi saw him, and when he stepped out of the Jeep he walked straight to the pickup truck. Hamza and Uzi both froze.

"What is your business here?" Prince Bader demanded of Uzi.

"Your highness…and…and excellency," Uzi stammered, "I…I have come to inspect the feathers…the feathers that doctor Jane repaired…the feathers of the falcon." He touched the stethoscope hanging around his neck.

"Do you know where the falcon is?"

"No, your highness."

"Then how are you going to inspect its feathers?"

"I thought it will be here."

"It is not here, so go back to the hospital."

"Yes, your highness."

"And if you see it, at the hospital or anywhere else, you call the Ahmadi Police Station and report that, understood?"

"Yes, your highness."

"Go!"

Uzi was only too happy to get out of there. He walked away without once turning to look back.

Prince Bader returned to the policemen. He exchanged words with one of them, then stuck his head inside the front Jeep and addressed Faisal Shahab.

"Where is your son?"

"I don't know," came the reply.

"I don't believe you."

Prince Bader stepped back from the Jeep and looked around him. He saw Hamza and Wadha, who was whimpering. He saw that there were a few inquisitive souls watching from the shadows, sensed that there were more he couldn't see.

Hamza heard him speaking to one of the policemen but couldn't hear what was said. Then he watched as the prince and two of the uniforms climbed into the Jeep that Faisal was in. It kicked up a cloud of dust as it sped off.

Wadha's whimpers became wails.

Chapter Nine

"Son of a whore!" Salman spat the words out with venom.

He was less than a mile from the tank farm, alternating between running and walking, his gait brisk, his *thobe* soaked through with sweat. He was thankful that bringing Hamza out to the tank farm yesterday had turned out to be a blessing, and not the risk he had subsequently feared it might be. It was also fortuitous that, fearing it was indeed a risk, he had decided not to bring Hamza to today's training session. Had he done so, the boy wouldn't have been in Magwa this morning, wouldn't have seen the police, and would not have been able to warn him and his father on their way home. The poor kid had been a mess when he'd flagged them down on the dirt road, breathless and near collapse. He had forced words out in fits and gasps to tell them what the police were doing, what they were saying.

Faisal had insisted on proceeding to Magwa alone, or at least without Salman, to assess the situation, see if it was safe for Salman to come home. Hamza had asked to remain with Salman, but had been overruled because he might be more helpful being in Magwa, as had just been demonstrated.

Salman didn't know what he was going to do. On the one hand, there was likely no better place to hide the *Sinjari* than inside one of the three unfinished tanks awaiting fabrication and installation of their roofs. That had been his father's idea, and Salman thought it brilliant. But they didn't know the construction schedule, so they didn't know how soon it would no longer be an option. Salman wondered if that even mattered any more. In hindsight, it had been foolhardy to think Prince Bader might agree to the citizenship proposition. Then again, he hadn't rejected it on the spot, so it must have been his uncle who had said no.

They were all sons of whores.

He knew from his father that the security guards at the tank farm mostly stayed in their air-conditioned hut and listened to a radio, venturing out only to check on vehicles seeking to enter the facility, or to raise the security barrier for those on the way out. The only times he had been past the gate were with his father. Now he wondered whether he should try to slip through unnoticed, or just tell the guards on duty that he was the son of their colleague, Faisal. But they would want to know why he wanted access.

His dilemma was solved when he got close enough to see that the chain link fence around the perimeter of the tank farm was just that, a chain link fence. The tops of the steel poles anchoring the fence had V-brackets, there to support barbed wire that would run along the top of the fence to prevent anyone from jumping over it. Salman had seen its like at other locations, and it was effective. Only here the barbed wire had not yet been installed. He was at a spot where he couldn't see anyone, and he hoped that meant no one could see him. He lifted his *thobe* and gripped its hem between his teeth, climbed up the fence and jumped over. The *Sinjari* was in the northernmost tank, the one nearest to him. To get to it he would have to traverse a stretch of ground where he would be out in the open, potentially visible to the construction crew. There was no alternative, so he ran. Half way across his fear was realized when two workers at an adjacent tank were in plain sight. He ran faster, reached his tank, and took the steps up its side in twos. He was still climbing when he heard the shout: "Hey!"

One glance over his shoulder confirmed that he had been seen. A construction worker was running towards him, another towards the entrance to the tank farm, presumably to the security office. Salman cursed under his breath and climbed as fast as he could until he reached the top and disappeared over the rim. He peered into the morning shadow at the base of the tank and saw his falcon atop his gear bag, a makeshift perch, hooded and serenely oblivious to the events unfolding around its sanctuary.

Salman scampered down the interior steps, grabbed the falcon and the gear bag and started back up the stairs again, only to realize it was too late. He heard the sound of heavy boots scrambling up the metal steps on the outside. He stopped, his eyes glued to the spot where the stairs met the rim. He grabbed the jesses around the falcon's ankles tightly and removed the hood from the falcon's head. A man wearing a construction hard hat appeared above him.

"What are you doing? Stop there!"

Salman didn't understand a word because it was in Filipino-accented English. He started up the stairs again. When he reached the rim, the Filipino tried to block him, but Salman pushed him aside. As he started his descent on the outside with the Filipino in tow, he could see the other construction worker and a security guard running towards the tank from one direction, and several other men from the Bechtel crew running towards them from another. By the time he reached the ground, he found himself surrounded by several men.

"What are you doing here?" the security guard demanded.

"I'm the son of Faisal Shahab, who works with you," Salman blurted out. "I was training my falcon when it flew over the fence and into the tank. I just came to recover it. No trouble. I am leaving now." He placed the hood over the falcon's head and tightened the braces.

Everyone's eyes were on the falcon.

"How did you get in?" the security guard said.

"I jumped over the fence. It was going to take too long to come around to the entrance. I didn't want the falcon to escape."

The guard relented. "Come with me, I will escort you out," he said.

The Bechtel men made way, and Salman followed the guard.

"I will tell your father about this," the guard said. "And I will report it to the company."

Salman was too relieved to argue, and too busy trying to figure out what to do next. He couldn't go to Magwa, not until his father returned and told him it was safe. That left one obvious choice. As soon as he was out of the gate he carried on towards the tree line of Ahmadi, less than a mile away to the south. He covered the distance in twelve minutes to a sandy berm on the town's perimeter. From there he had a clear view of the tank farm entrance. In the shade of large eucalyptus trees, he dropped his gear bag on the ground, set the falcon on it, and sat down to await the return of his father.

***

When Hamza saw the police take Faisal into custody, when he saw the police and Prince Bader drive off with Faisal in the back of the Jeep, his only thought was to get back to the tank farm to tell Salman what had happened, warn him to stay away. The policemen watching Magwa's eastern edge had already seen him leaving once that morning. To avoid raising their suspicion, he walked through the maze of shacks to the south and set off into the desert in full view of the Jeep parked on that side of town. When they approached him, he told the policemen the same story he had told the others earlier. A young boy on his way to answer nature's call was no cause for concern and, just like earlier, he was allowed to go. Once again, he walked until he disappeared behind the dunes, then he started running in the direction of the tank farm.

***

A policeman was driving, another sat in the back, next to a very grim-looking Faisal Shahab. Prince Bader was in the front passenger seat, staring straight ahead, barely able to contain his ire. They turned left on the road out of Magwa, southbound towards Ahmadi. It was also towards the tank farm. Faisal had no way of knowing if they had discovered the hiding place and were on their way there, or if they were taking him to the Ahmadi Police Station. A few minutes later he found out it was neither. When Prince Bader gave the word, the driver slowed down and turned right, off the road onto a dirt track that ran due west. Ten minutes later Prince Bader told the driver to stop.

They all got out of the Jeep. Faisal was ordered to sit on the ground. Prince Bader paced around him slowly. "Where is the *Sinjari?*" he said menacingly.

Faisal was torn.

The slap Prince Bader landed on Faisal's face toppled him over. The two policemen stepped closer, ready to tame Faisal if he resisted.

"Where is the *Sinjari?*" the prince barked.

"I don't know."

Faisal sat up and was slapped down again. This time he stayed down.

"I don't know!"

"Liar!" Prince Bader said. He exhaled an audible sigh of exasperation, stepped back, and reached into the Jeep.

"Sit up!"

Faisal sat up and rubbed his face.

Prince Bader turned back to him with a glass jar in one hand and a stick in the other. He crouched down and held the jar so Faisal could see what was in it. Faisal took one look and reeled back. The jar contained a two-inch long black scorpion, the venom of which he knew to be deadly.

"I drop this on the ground," Prince Bader said calmly, "it stings you, you have six, maybe seven hours. You'll be too weak to make it back to the road. But I will make sure you are found, and the cause of death will be easily established."

Fear drained the blood from Faisal's face. "I beg of you—"

Prince Bader started to unscrew the lid. "You want to play games with me, we'll play the scorpion game."

The lid came off.

"Stop, in the name of Allah, stop!" Faisal cried. "I will take you to the *Sinjari!*"

The lid went back on.

"Good. Let's go."

The policemen grabbed Faisal by his armpits and yanked him up off the ground. They pushed him into the back of the Jeep.

When they approached the road, Faisal said, "Turn right."

Prince Bader pivoted around from the front and looked at him. "To Ahmadi?"

"Not that far."

Prince Bader glared at him. "No more games!"

"No games," Faisal Shahab said, spent and defeated.

***

Hamza paced himself, adrenaline trumping his fatigue. He could see the road from where he was, and he thought about running to it and trying to catch a ride for the rest of the way, but no one ever stopped for him, so he pressed on. He guessed Salman would be with his falcon, in the tank, maybe even at the top of the tank, keeping a eye out for his father. He didn't know what was going to happen. Maybe when he learned that his father was in custody,

Salman would decide to just hand the falcon over to Prince Bader. Hamza thought that's what he would do. He hoped that's what Salman will do.

He could see the tank farm now. The wails of Salman's mother were still ringing in his ears. Why did women wail like that? It never helped, and it never solved anything, it just added an air of calamity when they did it, an air of doom.

He noticed a police Jeep on the road, heading south. He wondered if it was one of the Jeeps from Magwa. Maybe they had concluded that Salman and the *Sinjari* were not in Magwa. He saw the Jeep turn off the main road onto the feeder road that ran to the tank farm. Had they discovered Salman's hideout?

Ignoring the painful stitch that had developed in the side of his abdomen, he willed himself to run faster.

***

A guard saw the police approaching and raised the security barrier. The Jeep slowed down, and the driver waved to the guard who looked on in stunned disbelief when he caught a glimpse of Prince Bader.

"The *Sinjari* is inside one of the tanks," Faisal said.

"Inside a tank?" Prince Bader said. He would never have guessed. There was no end to the cunning of the *Bidoon*.

"One of the tanks still under construction," Faisal said.

"How do you get in?" Prince Bader asked, looking at the walls of the tanks.

"The steps. There's no roof yet."

"Which tank?"

"It's on the far side. Turn at the end of the row."

When the Jeep turned, Faisal pointed and said, "That one."

They came to a stop next to the tank. Prince Bader and the policemen jumped out of the Jeep and pulled Faisal out. They all faced the tank, their backs to the perimeter fence. None of them saw the boy who ran up to the fence on the outside and doubled over in pain, gasping for breath.

"Go up!" The prince ordered.

As Faisal started climbing the curved steps, Prince Bader followed close behind him. It was something he had to see for himself. The policemen stayed on the ground. Two construction workers began to approach, wondering what it was with the locals and that tank today. They stopped when a policeman waved them off.

Faisal wondered if Salman was in the tank with the falcon, wondered if his son could ever understand this betrayal. When he reached the platform at the top of the stairs and peered down inside the structure, he was shocked to see it was empty. Before he could react, Prince Bader hopped up onto the platform and saw the emptiness beneath them. His rage erupted as he turned on Faisal.

"I swear by the prophet Muhammad and—" Faisal stammered.

"Filthy scum!" Prince Bader thundered as he bore down on Faisal.

Faisal took a step back and raised his hands to ward off the blow, but still Prince Bader's open palm stung his face. He stepped back again and came up against the railing at the edge of the platform. He leaned away from Prince Bader's raised hand and lost his footing. In a split second of panic, he flailed his arms to avoid toppling over the railing. Prince Bader's second slap found its mark. The workers down below watched in horror as one of the two men at the top of the tank came over the railing, screaming as he plummeted in free fall, going silent when his body hit the ground with a sickly thud.

Hamza looked on, terrified. His physical pain subsided as fear overcame him. He slid down from his crouch to lie flat on the ground, his body numb.

Prince Bader realized the Bechtel men had witnessed what happened. He hurried down the stairs, shouting to the policemen to summon an ambulance. A policeman and the two construction workers were next to Faisal's motionless body. Blood trickled out of Faisal's mouth and dripped into a little puddle under his head.

"Terrible accident!" The prince said in English. He looked at the two Asians. "He slipped. I tried to catch him but he fell. You saw it, no?"

"I saw him falling," a Filipino replied. His co-worker nodded.

The second policeman shut the door of the Jeep and ran over.

Faisal moaned.

Prince Bader ordered everyone to step back. "He is alive! An ambulance is coming! We should not move him!"

"I will call my supervisor," the Filipino said.

"Stop!" said Prince Bader. "It doesn't help to have more people crowding over him."

The Filipino backed off.

"Have you been working on this tank?" Prince Bader asked.

"We are waiting for the roof to be fabricated."

"Has anyone been inside?"

The Filipinos exchanged a glance. "Just today there was a man," one of them said.

Prince Bader's eyes narrowed. "What man?"

"It was...maybe an hour ago...maybe less. He went into the tank and came out with a big bird."

The words jolted Prince Bader. So Faisal had brought him to the right place after all!

"Where did he go?"

"The security guard took him."

"Wait here for the ambulance," Prince Bader said to one policeman. To the other, "To the security hut."

In short order they were with the guard outside the guardhouse. "Which way did he go?" Prince Bader asked.

The guard pointed to Ahmadi. "He walked that way."

"And he had the hawk with him?"

"Yes."

"When you find someone trespassing in here, isn't it your job to detain him and call the police? What kind of guard are you?"

A fear-induced stutter crept into the guard's speech. "He said his hawk…flew in…and he collected it."

Prince Bader stared at Ahmadi and calculated his next move. He was getting closer, he could feel it. Somewhere in that town, Salman Shahab was in hiding with the *Sinjari*. But how to flush him out into the open? Sitting around waiting was not a good option. Ahmadi was much larger than Magwa. He would need at least twenty Jeeps to watch the perimeter, and he didn't have twenty Jeeps. Even if he did, deploying them would attract the attention of the wrong crowd. People would ask questions.

"If you see him again you detain him and immediately call the Ahmadi Police Station," he instructed.

"Yes, Master, you can trust me to do that," came the reply.

The ambulance approached the tank farm. Prince Bader waited until it passed them, then climbed into the Jeep. "To Ahmadi!"

***

Jane listened to Uzi with a growing sense of dismay and alarm.

"If Prince Bader had really trapped the Altai before Salman did, he would have told us that when he came here, but he didn't say a word. And if it were true, he wouldn't have offered to buy it from Salman, would he?"

Uzi had long since decided he didn't like Prince Bader, but he knew how powerful the man was and he was loath to take sides against him. He agreed with Jane but didn't show it.

"And why on earth would they take Salman's father away and leave his mother so distraught?" Jane added. "What the dickens is going on?"

She thought about her conversation with Zaig at breakfast, about the big picture and the little ones. She wondered what he would make of the morning's events in Magwa, the absurd claim by the police that the Altai belonged to Prince Bader, and the detention, or arrest, or whatever it was, of Salman's father. She felt a strong urge to call Zaig and share this information with him, but at this hour of the morning he would be seeing patients and wouldn't take kindly to being interrupted for this matter. Besides, it could wait till later because there was nothing either of them could do to help, even if they did decide to interfere in something that wasn't their business, which is exactly how Zaig would put it.

I won't let the little pictures cloud the big one.

Jane revisited the sentiment and decided it was easier said than done.

***

Salman was watching when the police Jeep turned off the main road and disappeared into the tank farm. He had no way of knowing if the guard had called the police to file a report after seeing him out, or if it was something to do with what was happening in Magwa. Could the police have forced his father to talk? Or maybe Hamza? He couldn't see who was in the Jeep, so he had questions but no answers. He was still watching a few minutes later when the Jeep reappeared and stopped at the guardhouse. He thought he could see some men moving about, but it was too far to be sure. He heard a siren, distant at first, then it got closer. He saw an ambulance on the main road, saw it turn off and race towards the tank farm. The ambulance disappeared past the guardhouse and the Jeep raced out towards Ahmadi.

He was itching to find out what that had all been about, but he didn't want to break his cover until he knew what was going on in Magwa. He held his nerve and bided his time in the hope it would not be long before he saw his father's white Datsun pickup truck coming down the road.

***

Paralyzed by the horror of what he had witnessed, Hamza waited until after the ambulance and police had left the tank farm before he got to his feet. He realized he was trembling. He didn't know where Salman was, but he knew he had to be either in the tank farm or somewhere close by. Hamza turned his back to the tank farm and walked due east, looking around, hoping Salman would see him, send him a signal, anything. He couldn't go back to Magwa now, because Salman was out here somewhere, and he had to warn him that he had to give Prince Bader the *Sinjari* or his fate would mirror that of his father.

He implored himself to think of what he would have done if he were Salman. He must have come back to the tank farm and taken the *Sinjari,* because it wasn't there anymore. Where would he have taken it? To a new hiding place, but where? The desert was vast, but it was open terrain. He looked around, and his eyes settled on the nearest cover, the trees of Ahmadi. Near enough for Salman to have walked to, dense enough for Salman to hide in, and close enough that Salman could see when the white Datsun returned to the tank farm. There was nowhere else. It had to be Ahmadi or Magwa, and it wasn't Magwa.

His fear hadn't subsided, but he was energized by a renewed sense of hope.

He set off towards Ahmadi.

***

Dr. Abdul-Razzaq Yassine was with a patient when an urgent call came through that an ambulance was heading to the hospital with a seriously injured local male. He quickly wrapped up the consultation and hustled over to the Emergency Room. He was told the inbound patient had fallen from a three-story height, was unresponsive, and had symptoms of severe internal injuries and trauma. When the ambulance arrived, the technician on board confirmed to the awaiting medical team that the patient still had a pulse. They wheeled him into the ER and got to work.

It was mid-afternoon when Zaig sat down to write the medical report. He noted that the patient in the critical care unit was one Faisal Shahab. He took pause to wonder why the name sounded vaguely familiar. A recent patient, perhaps? Someone in the news? His inability to place it was mildly irritating, but he let it go, thinking it could not be anyone or anything important.

Chapter Ten

The Ahmadi police station commanded a fleet comprising three yellow-and-black Mercedes-Benz W-108 police cars and eight charcoal grey Jeeps. Prince Bader had deployed five of the Jeeps in Magwa. By noon on Saturday he had sent the remaining three to patrol the streets of Ahmadi. He supplemented them with two of the Mercedes sedans, keeping the third at the station lest he needed to be driven somewhere.

He was sure Salman Shahab was in Ahmadi, because he was last seen walking towards the town from the tank farm, and because his only other options were Magwa or the desert. Of the three, Ahmadi, with its abundant trees, hedges and gardens, afforded the best cover. Sooner or later Salman would have to make a move, if nothing else, due to hunger. So the order was constant surveillance around Magwa's perimeter in case Shahab tried to return home, and, to the extent possible with the limited resources, in Ahmadi's interior.

The prince ate lunch at the police station, sandwiched between a joint of hashish for hors d'oeuvre and two lines of cocaine for dessert. He was psyched by the prospect of teaching Salman Shahab an important life lesson on the pecking order, as soon as the cops flushed the son of vermin out of whatever rat hole he was hiding in.

***

The police vehicles patrolling Ahmadi all had occasion to pass within twelve yards of Salman Shahab and his falcon, but none of their occupants were any the wiser for it. Their eyes were on the ground, on the bushes and hedges and the garden fences, and Salman saw them all from his vantage point high up in, and concealed by the leaves of, a stately eucalyptus tree. He had taken the precaution of removing his *thobe*, the white of which might betray him, and stuffing it in his gear bag while he played the cheetah hiding from the lion. He had set the falcon down on a limb above him, hooded and immobile, the gear bag dangling next to it. Outwardly he was still, but his mind was a whirlwind. He had seen police and an ambulance at the tank farm, and police patrols in Ahmadi, all of which left him certain that whatever was going on out there had to do with Prince Bader, and it wasn't good. But to find out what it was, he would to have to wait until nightfall, when the cover of darkness would enable him to move unseen back to Magwa.

Suddenly he tensed. Was that a whistle he had just heard? Faint, but familiar. He peered out as best he could through the leaves at the desert towards the tank farm. He heard it again, now louder, and there was no mistaking it. Hamza!

He slid down the branch to the trunk and lowered himself to the ground. He cupped his hands around his mouth and responded in kind. Two whistles later he saw the boy. He stood up, whistled one more time, and waved. Now Hamza saw him, and he came running. With a sense of foreboding, Salman climbed back up the tree to avoid being seen on the ground by one of the patrols. He had been expecting his father. The fact that it was Hamza who had come from Magwa was a worrying sign. When Hamza reached him, Salman told him to sit, to lean against the tree trunk, to keep his eyes on the road and not look up at him, to tell him in a low voice what had happened, and to stop speaking if a vehicle drove by.

Hamza recounted what he had seen and heard. Salman listened, asked a few terse questions, and pieced together in his mind the sequence of events. He felt guilt for having moved the falcon from the tank, and remorse for not selling the falcon to Prince Bader when the opportunity had first arisen. He thought about his father, timid and non-confrontational, and his mother, so fearful of the sons of whores. She had been right, of course. Had he listened to her, none of this would have happened, and his father would not be in the hospital. He glanced at the falcon and cursed the day it had come into his life.

"Go back home," he said to Hamza.

"I want to stay with you!"

"Go back the way you came. You are safe, they are not looking for you. If anyone stops you, say you are searching for a stray."

"What will you do?"

"I will wait until dark, then I will come home."

"And the *Sinjari*?"

"We will see."

"There are Jeeps around Magwa. They will see you."

Salman considered turning himself in, but he was not yet ready for that.

"Listen, Hamza," he said. "This is what I want you to do…"

***

The sun had not set when Jane Lambert's Wolseley pulled into the driveway at 23 12th Street, Ahmadi. It was a mild late afternoon, one that portended an even nicer evening, the agreeable temperature and low humidity combining to affirm that nature was cycling a new season in to replace the harshness of summer.

Zaig's Impala was not there yet. He must have either been delayed at the hospital, or he had swung by the *souq*, Ahmadi's valiant effort at a shopping center, to scratch his occasional itch to bring home the pick of the day's fresh produce.

Jane unlocked the front door and went to the kitchen. She grabbed a bottle of Pepsi Cola from the fridge, popped the top off, filled a tall glass, added ice, and savored the first sip. In the bedroom she kicked off her shoes and changed out of her medical scrubs into jeans and a loose-fitting shirt. She slipped her bare feet into a pair of Dr. Scholl's sandals. As she made her way to the living room she heard Zaig announcing his arrival with a toot of the Impala's horn, habitual whenever he got home and saw the Wolseley. She met him at the door, expecting there would be paper bags of fruits and vegetables that he needed help with, only to see it was not so.

"I thought you'd gone to the *souq*," she said.

"I was delayed at the hospital."

"Nothing serious, I hope?"

"There was an accident. A local man fell off one of the oil storage tanks at the tank farm."

"How terrible!"

"He's fighting for his life."

"I'm sorry, love." She gave him a hug. "And I thought my day was eventful!"

"How is that?"

Jane hesitated.

"New falcons?"

"No. A troubling development with Prince Bader."

Zaig sighed.

"We don't have to talk about it," Jane said. "You've had enough stress for one day."

"Tell me about Prince Bader."

"Well now he claims that *he* trapped the Altai falcon, and that it escaped from him before Salman Shahab trapped it, so he's claiming it belongs to him."

Zaig's eyes lit up.

"What?" said Jane.

"The man who fell off the tank today...last name is Shahab. Faisal Shahab. I knew it rang a bell."

They stared at each other. Jane thought of telling Zaig about what Uzi had seen, how Prince Bader and the police had taken Salman's father away, but she held back, preferring not to have to explain why Uzi had been there in the first place. When Zaig went to change his clothes, she called the falcon hospital and asked Uzi if he knew what Salman's father's name was. He didn't. She asked him to find out, to make one more foray into Magwa on the same premise as earlier and call her back as soon as possible. Then she sat back, thinking this could well be just a coincidence. She turned on the stereo and put an album on the turntable.

Zaig was outside, watering the grass, and Jane was restlessly leafing through a magazine to the strains of John Lennon singing about a man who blew his mind out in a car, when the telephone rang. She grabbed it, and went pale when she heard Uzi say, "Faisal." She went even paler when he reported that Salman's father had not come home since being taken away by the police.

As soon as Jane stepped outside, Zaig knew there were words behind her expression.

"Salman Shahab's father's name is Faisal Shahab," said Jane.

Zaig dropped the hose and joined her on the veranda.

"How do you know?"

"Uzi just found out from one of the Shahab's neighbors. What's more, the police picked him up in Magwa today, took him away in one of their Jeeps."

"Do we know it's the same Faisal Shahab?"

"How many of them can there be in this sliver of the world?"

Zaig didn't argue.

"I need to know, Zaig," Jane said. "I'm not sticking my nose in anyone else's business, but I need to know if the two Faisals are one and the same, and if so, how he came to fall off a tank when he was in police custody."

"Be careful, Jane."

"I have to know!"

He knew he was not going to talk her out of this, because he too wanted to know.

"Is there an address on the police report or admission form?" she asked.

"I didn't notice."

The music from the stereo gave way to the scratch of a stylus in a closed vinyl groove.

Zaig turned the stereo off and picked up the phone. With Jane watching by his side, he identified himself to the nurse at ICU and asked her to check Faisal Shahab's admission form for an address. It took a minute or so before the nurse came back on the line and reported that it contained just a single word: Magwa.

***

Salman waited until darkness had engulfed Ahmadi before he broke cover. He considered taking the falcon with him, but decided against it. If he got caught, and he had the falcon with him, it was over. But as long as they didn't know where the falcon was, he had a leg to stand on. He would sell the falcon to Prince Bader for the five hundred dinars that had already been offered, if the son of a whore was still game. If not…he wasn't sure what he would do.

He left the falcon hooded and tethered to the tree limb. He retrieved his *thobe* and left the gear bag in the tree, next to the falcon. He slithered down the tree, got dressed, and set off. He walked briskly to the northeast, instinctively steering clear of the lights of the tank farm's guardhouse. The stillness around him was pervasive, the silence absolute. Once clear past the tank farm, he cut back towards the west until he came to the dirt road he was so familiar with and followed it as it wound around the dunes towards his home.

Magwa had no electricity, but the falcon hospital did, and it had exterior lights, which were now his homing beacon. His first glimpse of them in the distance raised his spirits, and he picked up his pace. As he neared to within half a mile he heard the cough he had been listening for. He coughed back.

"Here!" Hamza's voice came through the darkness.

In a few seconds they were together.

"I got the *abaya*," Hamza said.

"May Allah bless you." Salman fumbled with the black cloth and draped it over his head and shoulders. "Hissa?"

Hamza made a clicking sound with his tongue. Salman held his breath in anticipation.

"You had us worried." Hissa's voice came from a few yards away.

Salman's heart fluttered at the sound of her voice.

"Allah be praised, I am fine," he said.

Hissa dropped her own *abaya* from her head to her shoulders and he made out the outline of her face.

"I am indebted to you," Salman said. "You will be in trouble if the police discover you helped me."

"I don't care," Hissa said. "Hamza, you go first, we will follow you."

Hamza started off along the track to Magwa. A swell of affection coursed through Salman, and he allowed himself the notion that Hissa had just intentionally orchestrated their being alone together for the first time. When she started to walk, he reached out and stopped her. She didn't protest.

He found her hand and caressed it. "You are my angel," he said. He couldn't see her blush, but she interlocked her fingers with his and squeezed.

As they walked towards Magwa, Salman knew from the lights of the falcon hospital exactly where they were. Presently Hissa let go of his hand and whispered, "The police are just ahead, on the right."

His plan, wearing an *abaya* and walking with Hissa, was for this moment. If the police stopped them and said anything, Hissa would answer, say she was with her mother, and they would hopefully let them pass. To his relief, they were neither stopped nor questioned.

His mother was waiting for him, having been told by Hamza that he was coming so she wouldn't act up when she saw him. She hugged him and peppered him with kisses and watched him devour the food she had prepared. The agony of her anxiety lifted when he told her he should have listened to her from the start.

"So go tomorrow morning and give Prince Bader the *Sinjari* and your father can come back home," she said.

He realized that she didn't know his father was hurt. He opted not to tell her.

"In the morning I will seek out Prince Bader," he assured her. "If he pays, fine, if not, so be it."

"It is Allah's will. These are not people we can challenge or defy."

"I understand that now."

"Praise be to Allah."

***

Jane voiced her suspicions to Zaig. He heard her out and conceded that something felt awry, but still he maintained that they could not interfere.

"What can we do?" he asked. "We can't interrogate Prince Bader!"

"I know, I know," Jane said, exasperation getting the better of her. "Can't you go to the tank farm, find out if anyone saw what happened?"

Zaig shook his head.

"What's a doctor doing coming to where the accident happened and asking questions? That a job for the police, not a doctor."

"I suppose you're right."

"Look," Zaig added, "Let's say something untoward happened out there, and let's say Prince Bader was involved. What could we possibly gain from poking our noses into it?"

Jane regarded him stoically. "It's Salman Shahab I'm worried about now."

Zaig understood, but that didn't change anything. "We can't get involved, Jane."

"I think this is a case of someone rich and powerful trampling all over someone poor and impotent. I can't stand myself for standing by and letting it happen."

"You are not letting it happen. If it's happening, it's not because of anything you're doing or not doing."

She eyed him defiantly. "I have to wonder if the Emir knows."

"What difference does it make?"

"If he doesn't know, maybe if he found out he would rein in his son and stop it."

"Are you proposing I speak with the Emir?"

Jane raised her eyebrows at him in a manner that told him she believed it might be the right thing to do.

It occurred to Zaig that there were times when communicating with her was futile, and this was one of them. He shook his head and turned away.

They didn't speak to each other again until a ringing telephone interrupted their sleep just before dawn. It was the hospital, informing Zaig that Faisal Shahab's vital signs had deteriorated perilously, and asking what might be done to save the patient's life. As he hurriedly got dressed, Zaig put his foot down and barred Jane from accompanying him. Then he scrambled to the hospital.

Chapter Eleven

There was only one waterbed in Kuwait, and it was the one Prince Bader bin Fahd Al-Dahem had shipped out from California at the end of his freshman year. It was of the free-flow single chamber variety, in which a disturbance of the water mass produces wave action that takes a few seconds to stabilize. Whenever he got into bed high, which of late was every time he got into bed, Prince Bader enjoyed the bobbing sensation resulting from any twitch or jerk of a limb. It wasn't so appealing when he awoke, for he found the motion prevented him from snoozing. So he had two beds in his room. His typical routine was to sleep through his stupor in the waterbed, and switch upon awakening to the regular bed for an hour or so of snoozing. As he was making that transition on Sunday morning, the bedside phone rang. He was not too groggy to remember that he'd left instructions with the police chief in Ahmadi to call him if there was any change of status, so he sat on the edge of the regular bed, rubbed his eyes, and answered.

"Good morning, Excellency," the voice on the line said.

"*Shaku?*" Prince Bader rasped.

"I just heard from the hospital that Faisal Shahab died."

"What about Salman Shahab?"

"Nothing new, Excellency."

"Spread the word in Magwa that Faisal Shahab has died of the injuries he suffered from an accidental fall. When the news reaches Salman Shahab, he will realize the stakes and come out of hiding like a dog with his head and tail down."

"Yes, Excellency."

There was no snoozing this morning, only a buzz in his bones. Prince Bader scratched his groin as he lumbered to the toilet. It was an auspicious start to the day.

***

Salman didn't have to walk to the nearest police Jeep to turn himself in on Sunday morning as he had planned, because the police came to him. He was still in the shack with his mother when it happened. A gruff voice from outside announced that there had been a fatal accident involving Faisal Shahab, and that the police were ready to transport next of kin to the Ahmadi Hospital so the body could be retrieved for burial.

Wadha lost it, started pummeling her chest with her palms. Her wails faded only when she fainted. Himself in shock, Salman was trying to revive her when Hamza's mother ran in, followed by Hissa. Salman exchanged a brief glance with Hissa, whose eyes aired desperation. She could see fear and anger in his, yet he somehow held it together. Eerily calm, he stepped outside.

"I am Salman Shahab," he said to the two stunned policemen, "the son of Faisal Shahab."

Hamza was in the crowd that had gathered, and he cared little that his tears were out in the open for all to see. The policemen jerked Salman's arms behind his back and handcuffed him.

"Leave him alone, bastards!" Hamza screamed as he ran at them.

One of the policemen grabbed Hamza and threw him to the ground while the other pushed Salman into the back of the Jeep. As an anguished wail emanated from the shack, several of the women in the crowd filed in to help with Wadha. The Jeep skidded around a corner with Hamza running after it, cursing manically and gesturing at the police to shove the whole of his right arm.

***

Jane was finishing a breakfast of omelet and buttered toast when she heard Zaig's car horn announcing he was back. She had lost count of the hours that had passed since he had left for the hospital, and her hope was that no news was good news. The first words out of Zaig's mouth when he found her at the dining table told her otherwise. "Bad news, I'm afraid."

Jane put her fork down.

"There was nothing we could do to save him."

Jane closed her eyes and let her chin drop. "He's dead?"

Zaig nodded.

"One of the policemen who brought him in was there. He confirmed that Faisal was Salman's father."

Jane took her plate into the kitchen, discarded the remnants of her food, rinsed the plate and left it in the sink. Zaig followed her into the bedroom. She was expressionless, but deliberate as she washed her face, brushed her teeth, and began to change into her medical scrubs.

"Where are you going?" Zaig asked.

She looked at him blankly, like he'd just asked a stupid question.

"To work. Where else would I be going?"

It was unlike her not to ask what he wanted for breakfast. He knew he couldn't get through to her when she acted this way, remote and disconnected from him. She picked up her car keys and purse and he followed her out the front door.

"Don't get involved, Jane."

She turned and looked at him. "In what?"

"Salman. Prince Bader. Whatever is happening in Magwa is not our business."

"Of course it isn't!"

He stood there and watched her as she got into her car and drove off without another word. She didn't even wave.

***

Another breakfast was interrupted that morning, this one some twenty-five miles north of Ahmadi, in the palace apartment of Prince Bader bin Fahd Al-Dahem, and the news was exactly what he wanted to hear. Salman Shahab had turned himself in and was being held behind bars at the Ahmadi Police Station. He felt a rush of gratification. He had been right, and his strategy had worked. This was vindication that erased all the frustrations of the past few days. When all was said and done, he would tell his uncle, Sheikh Mohammad, how easily he had outwitted and out-maneuvered the *Bidoon* boy. The natural order had prevailed. It was Allah's will.

A self-congratulatory celebration was in order. He stood out on a balcony overlooking the waters of the Gulf and smoked hashish. Then something occurred to him, something that made him frown. He stubbed the butt of the joint out in an ashtray, went back inside, and dialed a number on the phone. His anxiety built with every ring until the Ahmadi police chief answered.

"Do you have the *Sinjari*?" Prince Bader asked.

"No, Excellency. It wasn't with him when we captured him."

"Has he said where it is?"

"No, Excellency. But he acknowledges it is yours and says he will take you to it."

"I will be there in half an hour."

Prince Bader grimaced as he put the phone down. The *Bidoon* were not to be trusted. Surely the boy was not stupid enough to make things worse for himself? Surely he would know that defiance would only seal his fate?

He pushed a button on the intercom and ordered a police escort for his dash to Ahmadi.

***

Magwa was brimming with conjecture about what fate might befall Salman Shahab now that he was in the hands of the police. It was most distressing to Hamza, who was paralytic with dread. His sister shared his fear, and was weighed down with sorrow, but she couldn't bear to see Hamza in this state, crouched in a helpless funk outside the Shahab's shack, acting for the world to see like there was nothing worth living for.

"Don't just sit here, Hamza," Hissa said. "You know where the *Sinjari* is. Go see if it is still there."

There was only desolation in his heart, but Hamza's brain processed his sister's words. He pulled himself up, grabbed Hissa by the neck and kissed her forehead, then strode towards the dirt track. They had Salman, but they didn't have the *Sinjari!* If he could get to Ahmadi first, he could retrieve the *Sinjari* from the tree and hide it! He could singlehandedly foil Prince Bader! For the first time in his life, Hamza felt the vibes of empowerment. He felt no fear.

The police that had been watching Magwa's eastern perimeter were no longer there. Galvanized by the thought that he could, after all, help Salman's cause, Hamza started running.

***

The first thing that struck Jane as she approached Magwa was that the police Jeeps were nowhere to be seen. She didn't know what to make of that, but she smelled more trouble. When she reached the hospital, she told Uzi about Salman's father and again sent him to the Shahab's place to see what he could find out about Salman. He was gone barely fifteen minutes, and when he returned she knew from his expression the news was not good.

"Salman was taken by the police this morning," Uzi said.

It was a dreadful development.

"Taken where?" Jane asked.

"Nobody knows."

"Did he have the Altai?"

"No."

"Does anyone know where it is?"

"I don't know. I spoke to some of the neighborhood boys. Salman's mother is still there. She has just learned that her husband is dead. From outside the home I could hear her. She sounds like she is in shock and in distress."

Jane wracked her brain trying to think of what she could do to help Salman. Under the circumstances, business as usual at the falcon hospital was out of the question. Zaig wouldn't like this, but that was something she would have to deal with.

"Come on," she said to Uzi. We're going back there, and this time I'm coming with you."

"You are a good person, Dr. Jane," Uzi said as they walked into the slum. "And a brave person."

"I am a scared person, Uzi," Jane replied matter-of-factly. "I'm scared for Salman. When we get there, I'm going inside to try to talk to his mother. I'll need you to translate, so you stay at the entrance where you can hear and be heard but don't actually come in. You are a male; we must respect their customs."

Uzi was scared too, but he didn't show it. "A considerate person," he said.

There were several women in the shack with Wadha, and they were taken aback when Jane stepped in. None of them had ever been in the presence of a foreigner before, let alone a westerner.

Abayas were hastily pulled over heads, then allowed to drop back to shoulders when it became evident the foreign presence was strictly female.

"Assalamu alaykum," Jane said. The traditional Arab greeting was the first expression she had learned in the language.

A chorus of murmurings replied in kind. Jane immediately identified Salman's mother as the one in the center, the one too stricken to engage in social niceties.

"Uzi, please convey to Salman's mother my condolences. Tell her my husband is Abdul-Razzaq Yassine, the doctor who tried to save her husband's life at the Ahmadi Hospital."

When Wadha heard this from Uzi, her agonized gaze fell briefly on Jane.

"Tell them I know that Salman is innocent," Jane said. "Tell them I want to help. Ask if anyone knows where the Altai is."

Wadha shrieked when she heard the question. She moaned and uttered scorn.

"She curses the falcon for being the cause of her misery," Uzi said.

"I understand," Jane said, nodding sympathetically to Wadha. "Tell her if there is anything I can do to help, I can be reached at the falcon hospital."

Jane waited until Uzi translated before leaving the gathering.

"I understand why she feels that way towards the falcon," Jane said as she and Uzi walked away from the shack. "What first seemed like a wonderful stroke of luck for Salman has turned into a bloody nightmare."

***

The cell was stark. Concrete walls, a concrete floor and metal bars. A policeman who looked clueless but knew how to obey orders stood guard. Salman sat on the floor in his ankle-length underpants and his sleeveless undershirt. They had made him remove his *thobe* before pushing him into the cell. They had patted him down after they had handcuffed him in Magwa, so leaving him in his underclothes was not a security protocol. Salman had never been arrested before, and he wondered whether this treatment was standard, or whether Prince Bader had ordered it just to humiliate him. The answer came when they put another detainee in the cell with him, without first making him remove his *thobe*.

Salman felt no hatred for the policemen, not the ones who had brought him here, nor those staffing the station, like the pathetic soul guarding the cell. They were all just doing their jobs. His hatred was reserved for the invisible apparatus, the government who denied him fundamental human rights, the men who issued the orders, the untouchables who acted with impunity, and at the top of that pile, Prince Bader. He would be coming, there was no doubt about that, because he wanted the *Sinjari*. And after he got his hands on it, then what? Salman had no way of knowing whether he, too, would end up the victim of a fatal "accidental fall".

The other man in the cell asked the policeman to call someone for him, but his request was denied. Salman thought about how even if it was permitted, there was no one for him to call, because he didn't know anyone who had a telephone. Then he remembered he had seen one in the falcon hospital. Those were good people, the English doctor and her helper from Pakistan. He had sensed it when he took the *Sinjari* to them to repair the broken feathers. That now seemed like such a long time ago.

A metal door creaked open and clanged shut. The sound of boots on the concrete floor forewarned the guard that someone was approaching. It was another uniform, obviously a superior, for the guard saluted.

"Salman Shahab!"

Salman rose and stepped to the bars. His hands were still handcuffed behind his back.

"Come!"

The cell door was unlocked and opened. Salman stepped out and the door slammed shut behind him. The sergeant who had summoned him grabbed him by the shoulder and pushed him ahead.

"Watch yourself and behave with respect."

They went through several doors and corridors and into an interrogation room. Salman's throat was dry with fear, and every time he tried to swallow it seemed to get dryer. He had never before felt so exposed, so vulnerable.

"Where is the boy?"

It was Prince Bader's voice. Suddenly he was in the room, flanked by two policemen.

"Hello, Salman," he said with mock courtesy. "It has been a long time since we last met! How impolite of you to be so scarce!"

Salman's eyes were riveted to the glass jar in the prince's hand, to the creature inside it, a sinister-looking black scorpion.

Chapter Twelve

There was no way out for Salman, and he knew it. Prince Bader knew it too. But there was one thing of critical importance to him that he didn't know, and he set about addressing it without delay. He carefully placed the glass jar on the table in front of Salman.

"The last time you and I spoke was on Thursday. When I asked you where the *Sinjari* was, you said it was in a safe place. You said you wanted me to have it. You said it will be mine or you will release it to continue its journey."

Salman strained to maintain his poise. Everything Prince Bader had said was true.

"So now I ask you again, Salman, with no tolerance for oblique answers. Where is the *Sinjari*?"

Salman dropped his head and looked at the floor. "It is tethered to a tree in Ahmadi, master."

Prince Bader stared at Salman and narrowed his eyes as he assessed the response. It was the first time Salman had addressed him so deferentially. Amazing how fear sets people straight.

"You hid it in the tank farm before the tree?"

"Yes, master."

"When did you move it from the tank?"

"Yesterday."

"Why?"

"I was afraid the workers would find it. On Thursday I told you it was safe. I needed to ensure it stayed safe while I awaited your response to my proposal. I couldn't risk the workers finding it and releasing it."

Prince Bader nodded.

"It was unfortunate that your father slipped and fell to his death. A tragic accident."

Salman raised his eyes to meet Prince Bader's. He felt only rage and hatred for this man, yet he knew that at this time, in this place, he had to suppress both. He had a plan, but he had to stay in control of his emotions to have any chance of executing it. "Yes, master," he said.

"And now, in front of these witnesses," Prince Bader gestured at the policemen standing behind him, "do you acknowledge that I trapped the *Sinjari* before you did, and that it is rightfully mine?"

"How could I know that you trapped it first, Excellency?"

"Because I say it."

"Then it is true, master."

"And now it is time to return it to me."

"As you wish, master."

"Good."

"Master."

"What?"

"If you would see fit to give me the reward that you previously offered, for recovering your *Sinjari*…"

Prince Bader could hardly believe it. The audacity of the *Bidoon* boy! "That is for me to decide…after you return it."

"Of course, master."

Prince Bader took the glass jar off the table and waited until he saw that Salman's eyes were once again on the scorpion. "We don't want another accident, Salman," he said.

Any doubts Salman had that his father's fall had not been accidental vanished. "No, Excellency."

They rode out in a Mercedes and a Jeep, Prince Bader in the front passenger seat of the sedan, with Salman, still handcuffed, sandwiched between the two policemen in the back. Two more policemen followed in the Jeep. Salman told them the tree was one of those on the northern edge of Ahmadi. The problem was there were many fitting that description, and when they drove along Ahmadi's northernmost street, Salman lost his bearings.

"The trees and houses all look the same," he said. "Can we approach from the other side, from the desert?"

The policeman driving the Benz shook his head. "There is no road on the desert side," he said. He turned to Prince Bader and added, "We would have to go on foot, Excellency."

"No." Prince Bader turned to Salman. "We will drive back and forth slowly, and you will find the tree from here."

Salman knew he had to do it. They drove the length of the street twice, and still he couldn't identify the spot. On the third pass he looked the other way, in the direction he had faced when he was in the tree and watching the police vehicles drive past on the road. The tactic proved inspired, for this time he saw a combination of thatched fence, garden gate and carport that looked familiar. He looked across at the trees on the other side and thought he had found it. Then his heart skipped a beat. Was that Hamza he had just seen ducking behind the sand berm? What was he doing there? Salman was hit by a pang of panic. "Stop here," he said, hoping for all he was worth that the *Sinjari* was still in the tree.

The two drivers were ordered to stay with the vehicles while everyone else got out. A Kuwait Oil Company staff car driving past slowed down as the driver gawked at the sight of three policemen and a local official-looking type escorting a handcuffed prisoner in his underclothes across the street. One of the police drivers waved the curious onlooker on. Salman led the way, his heart pounding. He prayed that the falcon would still be in the tree, and that Hamza would lie low. As they neared the tree he was able to relax on the first count. There it was, perched right where he had left it. He couldn't point a finger at it, so he gestured up with his head. "There is the *Sinjari*."

Prince Bader stepped closer and peered up into the tree. He smiled with satisfaction.

"Good, good. How do we get it down?"

"I will climb and untie it and hand it down to you," Salman said.

Prince Bader considered the situation. The policemen were all armed and there were enough of them that it would be folly for Salman to try to escape. "Remove his handcuffs," he ordered.

When Salman's hands were free, he shook them for good measure, then proceeded nimbly up the eucalyptus trunk. Prince Bader and the policemen watched from below as Salman fiddled with the rope that secured the falcon to the tree. He positioned himself between the falcon and the gear bag. He also made sure that the men watching him from below could not see that he was actually tightening the knot instead of loosening it.

From his position behind the sand berm, Hamza watched with bated breath.

"What is the problem?" Prince Bader asked.

"I'm having difficulty untying this knot. I think I overdid it when I tied it. I wanted to be sure it was secure. Just a minute."

Salman reached for the gear bag and lifted it onto his lap. He pulled out the leather cuff and let it drop to the ground below. Banking on that momentary distraction, Salman took his dagger out of the gear bag and stuck it in the waistband of his underpants, quickly covering the handle with his undershirt. Hamza saw this and thought Salman was going to use the dagger to free the falcon.

"I will need the cuff," Salman said.

Prince Bader motioned to one of the policemen, who picked the cuff up off the sand and tossed it up towards Salman. It was a bad throw, but the second attempt was on target and Salman caught it. As he reached to do so, his gear bag fell to the ground.

"That's alright. I don't need the bag."

He continued to twist and turn the rope, acting like he was trying to untie it.

Prince Bader was getting restless. He was so close to the *Sinjari* he wanted it in his hands. "Still can't untie it?" he asked testily.

"It is no use," Salman said. "My wrists are sore from the handcuffs. This is too painful."

Prince Bader's impatience got the better of him. "Let me see," he huffed.

He lifted his *thobe* and tied the hem around his waist, then started to climb up the tree, sticking close to how Salman had ascended. When he heaved himself up onto the limb next to Salman and the falcon, he got his first clear view of the knot that Salman had been so occupied with. He tried to untie it. Salman watched calmly and rubbed his wrists.

One of the policemen murmured to his colleagues that he thought Prince Bader was too close to Salman, that he was too exposed to being pushed. "Excellency," he started.

"Wait!" was the terse reply.

"May Allah prot—"

"I need a knife, something sharp!" Prince Bader said irately.

"Take this one!"

In the time it took Salman to spit the words out he was already landing the first stab of his dagger deep into Prince Bader's neck. Blood squirted out as Salman stabbed again and again.

Hamza watched in stunned disbelief.

The reaction of the policemen under the tree was delayed by shock. The other two by the road couldn't see what was happening, they only knew something was awry when they saw Prince Bader fall from the tree, his white *thobe* soiled by blotches of blood. All five policemen trained their handguns on Salman and barked at him to drop the dagger and come down. With glazed eyes, Salman eased himself to the ground.

Hamza peeked over the berm at the bedlam. Two of the policemen shoved Salman to the ground and rained blows on him with their fists and boots. He was in the fetal position, his hands covering his head. The police forced his hands behind his back and handcuffed him again. The beating continued while another policeman picked up the limp body of Prince Bader and laid it in the back seat of the Mercedes. The car burned rubber as it screeched off, siren wailing and lights ablaze. The policemen lifted Salman, now battered and bleeding, dragged him to the Jeep, threw him in the back and drove off.

Hamza slid back down behind the berm, shuddering uncontrollably. Traumatized by the harrowing scene he had just witnessed, he sprinted frantically into the desert, desperate to get back to the familiar confines of Magwa.

Chapter Thirteen

The news spread through Kuwait faster than a midsummer S*hamal* sandstorm.

It rippled first through the Ahmadi Hospital after two panicky policemen delivered Prince Bader's body, dead on arrival, the cause of death obviously massive loss of blood resulting from multiple stab wounds. Dr. Abdul-Razzaq Yassine was as stunned as anyone by the identity of the victim, and his shock was compounded when he learned from the police that the perpetrator of the hideous crime was Salman Shahab, son of the Faisal Shahab that had expired at the hospital in the darkest hours of that very same morning. His recent conversations with Jane came to mind, in particular his pleas that she not get involved in an affair that was not their business. How was it she had described what she thought was happening? The powerless against the omnipotent, or something like that? What would she say now?

He would call her and tell her in due course, but first he had to attend to the formalities of the terrible situation at hand. The demise of Faisal Shahab was a Friday stroll on the shores of the gulf compared to this.

A few miles away, the Ahmadi police chief erupted in a rage fueled by fear; ire at the imbeciles on his staff who had let the atrocity happen, fear because he knew his superior in Kuwait City would lump him in that same category. The stark truth was it had happened in his territory, on his watch. His voice was quivering when he made the call and told his boss what had happened. It didn't help that the head of Kuwait's police force was himself of the ruling Al-Dahem clan, so a cousin, albeit a distant one, of Prince Bader. He in turn reported to the minister of the interior, another cousin, and a half-brother of the Emir. Within minutes, the devastating news reached the ear of the Emir.

When he heard he had lost his only son, the Emir's reaction was disbelief, denial and anguish. Moments later the palace press secretary notified the state-run broadcast media, and the country's radio station switched to live readings from the Quran. Kuwaitis of all stripes adored the Emir. His loss was felt as theirs. The widespread outpouring of grief was visceral and unrestrained.

While there was no electricity in Magwa, a few in the community owned battery-powered radios. Word of mouth quickly informed the rest. A new scrum of dwellers gathered outside the Shahab's shack. Despite the efforts of some of the women to shield Wadha from this latest bombshell, she caught wind of it. What had previously been angst now became hyperventilation, paranoia and panic. She started keening, slapping herself, pulling her hair. Only Hissa, the neighbor's daughter, had the presence of mind to think of calling the English doctor. She stepped outside and was almost accosted by a frenetic Hamza.

"I witnessed it," he said, "I saw everything, everything!"

She had never seen him so frenzied. She pulled him aside, away from the throng.

"Witnessed what?"

When he started telling his sister what he had seen, stuttering as he did so, she took his hand and pulled him along with her.

"Come, we must get the English doctor because Wadha is going crazy! You settle down, I don't want you to go mad too!"

As the siblings hurried towards the Quonset hut on the ridge, Uzi answered a ringing telephone and informed Jane that it was her husband on the line. The color drained out of Jane's face as she listened to Zaig recount what had transpired. It was stupefying news, overwhelming, and she was having a hard time processing it.

As Zaig told her he was being summoned anew and had to go, Uzi walked into the room with Hissa and Hamza.

Jane listened with barefaced astonishment at Hamza's bewildering barrage of details. He went back and forth between what he had witnessed yesterday at the tank farm, and what he had seen this morning in Ahmadi. Hissa let him talk, as he had settled down some and she was hearing details for the first time. Uzi translated when necessary, his own mind boggled by the boy's testimony.

Jane distilled everything down to the horrifying facts. Prince Bader was dead, murdered by Salman. Appalling, but apparently the ugly truth. Faisal Shahab was dead, accident or otherwise, a tragedy in its own right now almost forgotten in the maelstrom that had ensued. Salman had been badly beaten by the police, and he was in their custody. Her heart still went out to him, but there was nothing she could do.

"Has Wadha been told?" Jane asked.

The name was a trigger for Hissa, who suddenly remembered why she had wanted to come here in the first place. Jane heard her out and responded that yes, there was medication she could give Wadha, something that would sedate her, but she would have to fetch it from Ahmadi. She would make haste and be back within half an hour, a quick stop at the Ahmadi hospital to get something for Wadha from Zaig.

As she got up, something else suddenly occurred to her. The exchange had all been about Salman and Prince Bader and Faisal and the police. A central figure in the drama had gone virtually unmentioned. "Do you know where the falcon is?" Jane asked Hamza.

The boy's eyes grew wide. "It was in the tree in Ahmadi. I saw it."

"Is it still there?"

"It was there when I left."

Jane turned to Uzi. "You, me and the boy, to Ahmadi, now. The young lady waits for us here. We'll get medication for Salman's mother, and we'll retrieve the Altai." She added under her breath, "If it's still there."

Jane set a personal speed record on the way to Ahmadi, and she went to the hospital first. She found Zaig on the first floor, in the clinic where he saw patients.

"I need a sedative to give to Salman's mother. Sounds like she's having a nervous breakdown."

"Did you go and see her?"

"No. One of the women came to me and asked if there is anything we can do. We need a medical response. Nothing personal."

Zaig relented and handed her two syringes and a couple of vials from a secure cupboard. "Be careful!"

Jane ran back out to the car. On the way in from Magwa, Hamza had pointed to the area on the perimeter where everything had happened, and Jane knew they would have to access it from the northernmost road in Ahmadi. She slowed down when she thought they were in the vicinity. Hamza soon spotted Salman's gear bag where it had fallen from the tree.

Jane and Uzi followed Hamza and looked up when he pointed into the tree. The hooded falcon was still serenely poised where Salman had left it. It took Uzi but a few seconds to scale up the tree and reach it. He quickly realized that the knot in the rope securing the falcon to the tree limb was so tight that untying it was going to be a challenge.

"I need to cut through the rope."

Hamza looked around and spotted Salman's bloody dagger on the sand.

"Here's Salman's knife!" He started towards it.

"Don't touch it!" Jane warned.

"I don't need it, I have one," Uzi said. He had already pulled his keychain out of his pocket. Now he pulled open the blade of the small penknife amongst his keys. The blade was only two inches long, but that was enough. He sawed through the rope. Hamza found Salman's cuff on the sand next to the gear bag and tossed it up to Uzi. It was a trick getting down with the falcon on his hand, and Uzi lost his footing and slipped down the last two yards, but the soft sand broke his fall.

"Leave everything where it is," Jane said, eyeing the dagger and the gear bag. The three of them hustled back into her car. A quick U-turn and they were heading back towards the road to Magwa.

"You are not to tell anyone that we took the falcon from the tree," Jane said sternly. "If you do, we could all be in trouble."

Uzi ensured that Hamza understood, and the boy nodded in agreement.

Hissa was waiting outside the hospital. The warning was repeated to her, and she too confirmed that she understood. Uzi took the falcon into the hospital as Jane, Hissa and Hamza set off for Magwa.

It was a predictably shambolic scene inside the Shahab's shack, although Wadha appeared to have tired herself out some. The women held her down and Hissa exposed an upper arm. Jane filled a syringe with fluid from a vial. A quick tap and squirt and the needle was in Wadha's arm. A few moments later, to audible collective relief, she succumbed to the sedative.

Back at the hospital, Jane performed a thorough physical examination of the falcon. All appeared well but for some weight loss that Jane attributed to insufficient nourishment. When Uzi fed her, the falcon displayed a reassuringly healthy appetite. Jane wondered what kind of risk she was taking by removing the falcon from the scene of a crime and bringing it to the hospital. Not just any falcon, *this* one, the Altai. She believed it belonged to Salman, but she had no notion of holding it in safekeeping for him because it was unlikely he would ever set eyes on it again. And the other interested party, Prince Bader, was dead, along with whatever crooked schemes he had conjured up to make the falcon his. But she couldn't have left it sitting in the tree. Hooded and tethered, it would have perished. Retrieving it had been the humane thing to do. Still, she didn't know what legalities might come into play, and that was now a concern. She placed the falcon in a locked interior room with no windows. She put off any further decisions until after the dust settled in the coming days.

***

The motorcade that descended on the Ahmadi Police Station comprised seven cars, their occupants representing the best crime-investigation expertise Kuwait had on tap. All the men wore surly expressions, none more so than Sheikh Mubarak Al-Dahem, head of the country's police force, a man whose authority was underscored by the same family name as that of the Emir and, more poignantly on this day, that of the deceased prince. Over the course of several hours he listened, queried, coaxed and cajoled every member of the force that had been involved in Prince Bader's Magwa escapades over the previous few days. At one point he put the inquisition on hold while he took a call. It was from his uncle, the Prime Minister, Sheikh Mohammad, who apprised him of the two conversations he had had with Prince Bader, the first in person last Thursday at his *diwaniya*, the second by telephone the following day. By mid-afternoon Sheikh Mubarak had pieced together an understanding of the circumstances and timeline of events leading up to the fatal attack in the tree. It was clearly a premeditated killing, a hideous crime for which the *Bidoon* boy would pay with his own life. He also took one look at the criminal, and was repulsed by the sight of him. The prisoner's face was grotesque, two black eyes, one of which was swollen shut, the nose broken, the lips bloodied. That in addition to an assortment of ugly bruises. All deserved, of course, but a potential embarrassment if publicized for what it spoke of police brutality. Sheikh Mubarak spat on the ground. He issued an order to have the Kuwaiti Dr. Yassine from the local hospital come to the police station and do what he could to clean up the mess.

There remained just one issue unresolved. The whole nasty business revolved around a *Sinjari* falcon, the fate of which nobody had elaborated on. Sheikh Mubarak asked the question. The realization dawned on everyone in attendance that the raptor had last been seen at the scene of the crime. Sheikh Mubarak led the team of investigators back to the tree. They found the *Bidoon* boy's gear bag and his dagger, still stained with blood. But apart from droppings in the sand, there was not a trace of the falcon.

Sheikh Mubarak recycled a question and was told that the falcon had definitely been hooded, an assertion corroborated by all five policemen who had witnessed the crime. His final word on the matter before heading back to the police station was as terse as it was indisputable. "Hooded falcons don't fly."

***

Jane didn't see Zaig again until that evening, when he got home after what had been a draining day. He poured two black market Johnny Walker Red Label scotch and sodas and took them into the living room.

"Now you see why I didn't want you to get involved," he said as he handed Jane a glass. "I didn't think anything like this could happen, but I knew there was nothing to be gained for you or us by interfering, regardless of motive."

They both swallowed large gulps of the whiskey.

"What's going to happen to Salman?" Jane said.

"He will be sentenced to death."

Jane grimaced. "It is a cruel world we live in."

"Indeed. There was no shortage of cruelty in the way Prince Bader was butchered."

The last thing Jane wanted to do now was argue. She took another swig of her drink.

"Yesterday you said you were worried about Salman Shahab," Zaig continued. "I must say now I am worried for the whole *Bidoon* community, because of Salman Shahab."

It was something that hadn't occurred to Jane. "Do you think there will be a backlash against them?"

"I don't know. Emotions are bound to run high. There was already antipathy towards them, and this was a gruesome act."

"Forgotten in all of this is the fact that Faisal Shahab is also dead and may himself have been murdered," Jane noted.

"Yes, I'm afraid you're right, that is forgotten now."

"I'll tell you who I feel for most of all," Jane said, "Salman's mother. The poor woman has lost her husband, and now she's going to lose her only son."

"Speaking of only sons, let's spare a thought for the Emir. He, too, has lost his."

Jane felt the first effects of the whiskey, a warming in her gut. "True. But Prince Bader was one of three victims of a series of events that he instigated."

"We don't know that for sure, Jane. What if Prince Bader really did trap the falcon first?"

"He didn't. If he had done, he would have said something about that to me when he came into the hospital last Tuesday. And he didn't say anything about that to Salman. And if that really was the case, he wouldn't have offered to buy it from Salman."

"I don't think any of that is necessarily true or conclusive."

"That's because you are biased."

"Really?"

"Yes. You are protective of the establishment, of the Emir and of Prince Bader. In your eyes they can do no wrong."

"And in your eyes, everything they do is wrong! You condemned the Emir based on some woman's gossip you heard at the club!"

"Enough, Zaig, please. Let's stop now. We both know we don't see eye to eye on what's happened here, but we're not going to get anywhere arguing about it."

Zaig was relieved that he hadn't told Jane that he had seen, and had tended to, Salman Shahab at the police station that afternoon. For her part, Jane was relieved that she hadn't told Zaig that she had seen, and had tended to, Salman's falcon that afternoon, and that she was now the custodian of the contested creature. At that moment, the two of them would have said *Ameen*—Amen to one sentiment: Some information is best not shared with a spouse.

Chapter Fourteen

The new season's first cold front swept through Kuwait during the pre-dawn hours on Monday, driven by a cooler, dryer wind than had been seen since March. It cleared the air, adding radiance to the moon, but it failed to lift the deflated mood in the land as Kuwaitis awoke to sobering news: One Salman Shahab had confessed to the aggravated murder of Prince Bader, a crime punishable by death. The Emir had granted his approval, clearing the way for an execution by hanging on Tuesday.

Zaig was shaving when he heard the news on the radio. He instinctively nodded. Justice was best served swiftly. He mentioned it to Jane as they ate breakfast. She lost her appetite and left the table. The image of Salman hanging from a noose was unbearable. Her heart went out to Salman's mother, and only to Salman's mother. Jane wondered how the woman was doing. The effects of the sedative she had injected her with would have worn off by now. Had she heard today's news? Sweet Jesus, how was she going to cope with that? How would she ever find closure?

Jane was too depressed to go to work. She decided she would only drive to Magwa if Salman's mother needed another shot, otherwise she would stay at home. She was thinking she needed to call Uzi, when the telephone rang. Zaig was still eating, so Jane answered it. To her surprise, it was Uzi.

"I was just about to call you," Jane said. "Is everything alright?"

"Yes, Dr. Jane. It is Salman's mother."

"What about her?"

"She is here."

"At the hospital?"

"Yes. She wants to see you."

"Is she alright?"

"Yes. She asked me to call you. She wants to see you and Dr. Yassine."

"Zaig?"

"Yes. The two of you."

"Does she need more medication?"

"She doesn't seem to need more medication. She is calm."

"She is calm?"

"Yes, calm."

"How odd." Jane wondered if Wadha had heard the news. Uzi probably hadn't heard either, but this was not a good time to tell him. "Hold on, Uzi."

Jane put the handset down and went to the dining room.

"Uzi's on the phone. Salman's mother is at the hospital, and she's asking to see us."

Zaig wiped his mouth with a napkin. "Us?"

"Yes."

"Why us?"

"I don't know. Do you want to talk to her?"

"Not particularly."

"Zaig. Please. It could be a medical issue."

Zaig slid his chair back and stood up. "Is she on the phone?"

"Uzi is. I'll have him put her on."

They walked to the entry hall and Jane picked up the handset. "Uzi, can you put her on the phone? Zaig will speak with her."

Zaig took the handset. This was most unexpected. "Yes?"

"Doctor, I am Wadha, Salman Shahab's mother."

"I know who you are."

"I want to see you. Please come to Magwa."

Zaig was struck by how assured she sounded.

"What is the problem?"

"I beg of you, come to Magwa."

"Now?"

"Yes. There is no time to lose."

Zaig was uncomfortable with the request. Jane was looking at him with questioning eyes. He couldn't decline. "Stay where you are. We will be there in fifteen minutes."

He put the handset back on its cradle. "Very strange. Let's go and see what she wants."

They found Wadha standing outside the hospital entrance in her black *abaya*.

Jane wondered if this had anything to do with the falcon. Had Hamza or his sister said anything? She braced herself, because if so, Zaig was not going to be impressed.

After a brief exchange of greetings, the three of them stepped inside. Uzi was behind the reception desk in the foyer. Wadha kept the *abaya* covering her hair, but she showed her face. Jane thought she looked remarkably poised, considering.

"Please thank your wife for me," Wadha said to Zaig. "The medicine she gave me helped."

"Do you need more?" Zaig asked.

"No."

"What did you want to see us for? Just to give thanks?"

"No."

Zaig waited.

"You heard the news today?" Wadha asked.

"Yes," said Zaig.

"I want to speak with the Emir. I want to ask him for clemency."

Zaig was taken aback. "What does that have to do with us?"

"You are the only people I know who can arrange for him to meet with me."

"What makes you think that?"

"He knows you, and he knows your wife. He established this falcon hospital. Either you or she can reach him. I can't. You are my only hope."

Jane had understood most of the conversation. Zaig gave her the gist of it in English just in case. They both thought it was an astonishing request. Uzi remained silent.

"Impossible," Zaig said to Jane. "I won't do it."

"Yes, it is a bit of a stretch," Jane agreed. "Still, you can't fault her for wanting to try to save her son."

"The Emir will not grant clemency. Not for the murder of his son!"

Zaig switched to Arabic and repeated the words to Wadha.

"I want to speak with the two of you alone," Wadha said. She glanced at Uzi.

Jane ushered Wadha and Zaig into another room, followed them in and closed the door.

After a few minutes the door swung open and the three of them filed back into the foyer in silence. Jane made a telephone call to a man whose name Uzi recognized as the liaison between Jane and the Emir on all things to do with the hospital. When they needed something, equipment, supplies, whatever, he made it happen. Jane told him she needed to see the Emir today, his Excellency's tragic personal circumstances notwithstanding. She emphasized that it was a matter of the utmost urgency. Then Zaig placed a call, and it sounded to Uzi like Dr. Yassine was talking to his father, asking him to contact someone he knew, someone apparently influential, someone who could arrange for an audience with the Emir. There was a reference to the terrible news that had saddened all of Kuwait. Thereafter Zaig made one additional call and arranged for someone to cover for him at the Ahmadi Hospital. Jane advised Uzi that he was not to expect her back today. The three of them left in the KOC Impala, Zaig behind the wheel, Jane next to him, and Wadha in the back seat.

It was mystifying to Uzi how a woman who had just lost her husband and was about to lose her only son, a woman whose anguished wails had yesterday sickened all who heard them, could now be so calm.

Chapter Fifteen

A profound sense of incredulity underpinned the thoughts swirling around in Jane's mind. It was exactly—almost to the hour—one week since Salman Shahab had walked into the hospital with his falcon, unleashing a sequence of events so bizarre, Jane could never have scripted them. The vagaries of life could amuse and amaze, but the situation at hand beggared belief. She wanted to console the poor woman sitting in the back seat, to hold her and protect her, but the only thing she could do for her was what she and Zaig were doing, use whatever leverage they had to get her an audience with the Emir. Yet the pity Jane felt for Wadha was surpassed by the awe with which she regarded her resilience. With all she had been through, the stress and anguish, she still was able to hold it all together. Even now, despite the occasional sob and murmurings about Allah's will, Wadha was doing remarkably well. Just as well, Jane thought, for she would need to be strong when she faced the Emir. Once again, the dichotomy the Altai affair had dished up came to mind, the way it had pitted against each other the two extremes of Kuwaiti society, first Salman and Prince Bader, and now, this.

Zaig, too, was lost in his thoughts. For all his entreaties to Jane not to get involved in an affair that didn't concern them, here he was taking Wadha Shahab to see the Emir. He knew it was the right thing to do, for only the Emir could approve an execution, and only the Emir could grant clemency. He minded the traffic and wondered how the coming hours would play out.

The national flag atop the palace flew at half-mast. Zaig was relieved that the guards had already received word from inside and were expecting them, for it meant strings had been pulled to good effect.

A solemn air pervaded the interior of the palace; what few words were spoken were uttered in hushed tones. Jane and Zaig both hoped they wouldn't see the Emir. What do you say to a man whose son had just been murdered? They felt relief when they were politely asked to take seats in an outer chamber, while Wadha was invited through another door that was then softly closed.

Wadha found herself in an ornately-furnished anteroom with a large desk attended by the Emir's personal aide. The only other door in the room was manned by an armed uniformed member of the elite Emiri Guard. When Wadha entered, the aide rose and disappeared through the door. A moment later he reappeared and held it open for Wadha. She shuffled nervously into the Emir's office, holding her *abaya* so that it covered everything but her eyes.

The Emir sat behind his desk, looking older than in any of his official portraits. And unlike in the portraits, he did not smile.

Wadha heard the soft click of the door closing behind her. She glanced around and saw that it was just the two of them. He didn't ask her to sit down, so she stood before him, aware that she could not stop trembling.

"My condolences, Excellency," she said, her voice barely louder than a whisper.

He nodded. "And my condolences to you, for I understand you have lost your husband."

There was a heavy silence as she searched for words.

"I understand you are here to plead for clemency for your son," the Emir said. "It is my duty to hear your plea."

"Enough death, Excellency."

He regarded her stoically. "I set aside the personal dimension, for it would cloud any man's judgment. The circumstances of the crime are beyond question, the witnesses many, the body of my son irrefutable testimony to the viciousness of the attack. I also consider the weight of public emotions, which run high, and the ramifications of my decision on the country's stability, on law and order. All taken into account, there is no possibility of clemency. May Allah have mercy on your son's soul."

Wadha swallowed hard and willed herself to be strong. "Our son," she said.

The Emir let the words hang for a few moments, his eyes locked on hers.

She lifted her *abaya* from her head and dropped it to her shoulders, exposing fully her face and her hair.

The Emir narrowed his eyes.

"You may not remember, but I was sixteen years of age when you married me for two nights, eighteen years ago."

He was unmoved. "You are fantasizing," he said dourly.

"Shall I describe to you what is between your legs?"

The Emir flinched.

"Salman is your prisoner. You can strip him naked and see for yourself that intelligence and compassion are not the only traits of yours that the creator has endowed him with."

The Emir's expression slowly softened. "I remember you," he said, nodding wistfully. "I remember you, Wadha. But what about your husband?"

"Mine was a marriage of convenience to an impotent man. No untarnished woman would take him, and after I realized I was pregnant, I knew no complete man would take me. We were the only chance either of us had."

The Emir was visibly stunned. "And how did you explain to him your child?"

"I told him I had been married, and that the marriage didn't last. It is the truth, no? He accepted that my pregnancy was not a matter of dishonor. He asked, but I didn't tell him who, and he never asked again. He raised Salman like he was his boy. But you are the only man who ever touched me. Salman is your son."

After what seemed like an eternity, Sheikh Fahd bin Khaled Al-Dahem rose from his chair and gestured to the sofa. "Please, Wadha, sit down. I beg of you, relax."

Epilogue

A man was hanged in Kuwait during the first week in October 1968, having been convicted of drug trafficking a few weeks earlier. He was brought to the gallows with a burlap sack covering his head, in an event that was closed to the public. A press release issued by the Ministry of the Interior, and carried by Kuwait's print and broadcast media, asserted that with the execution, the killer of Prince Bader bin Fahd Al-Dahem had been brought to justice. The citizenry as one praised the might of right.

***

Shortly thereafter, a civilian Mercedes-Benz sedan with four passengers pulled up on the Kuwaiti side of the customs and immigration post at the border with Saudi Arabia. The documents presented were authentic Kuwaiti passports, the numbers of which had been processed for permanent residency in the kingdom in an extraordinary agreement made between the very highest authorities in the Kuwaiti and Saudi governments. They bore the names and photographs of Salman Al-Obaid, his wife, Hissa, his mother, Wadha, and his brother in law, Hamza. They passed through the border without ado, on their way to start a new life in a new country.

***

That same afternoon, anyone watching the Quonset hut atop the ridge to the north of Magwa would have seen a magnificent falcon take to the skies. It was in perfect health and not at all hungry. It would have taken a very keen eye, and more than passing knowledge of the raptor world, to discern that it was of the species *Falco cherug altaicus,* more commonly known as an Altai Saker.

***

A few days later, Dr. Abdul-Razzaq Yassine beheld his wife quizzically and remarked that the only remaining loose end in the Altai affair was the whereabouts of the falcon at the center of it all. She met his gaze with practiced sangfroid, then crossed her heart and told him, truthfully and cheerily, that she had no earthly idea where the falcon was.

Acknowledgments

J. David Remple, BA, DVM, was the founding director of the world's first hospital for hunting falcons, established in Dubai in 1983. He graciously gave of his time to answer my questions about falconry in general, and the nuances of Arabian falconry in particular. He returned to his native Colorado after nearly two decades in the UAE. His personal account of his time in the Middle East is titled *Footprints on the Toilet Seat – Memoirs of a Falcon Doctor*. He is also an artist. His rendition of a falcon illustrates the front cover of this book. Thank you, David.

Thanks too to another David, David Ruiz, for the back cover photograph.

I might well be adrift and at the mercy of high seas were it not for the anchor and rudder of love, encouragement and support of family and friends. Topping the list, of course, Rana.

Printed by Amazon Italia Logistica S.r.l.
Torrazza Piemonte (TO), Italy